WILD RIDERS

They were the last of the Rebel raiders—burnt-out, bitter, starved for vengeance. Hunted outlaws, they swore to fight to the last round against the Yankee rule in Missouri.

Brade Bradenton was a law-abiding man—until he returned from the war to find everything he owned brutally destroyed. Now he rode with the raiders, hating the violence, but knowing justice comes only at a high price.

One day a man named Logan came to Bradenton with a plan to smash the Yankees; all he needed was money—the kind of money the banks only give out at gunpoint.

Lee Hoffman was born in Chicago, Illinois, and attended Armstrong Junior College in Savannah from 1949 to 1951. During her first college year she discovered science-fiction fandom and the vast network of correspondence and amateur publishing that it supported. She made many friends in this new world and even founded her own monthly magazine, *Quandry*, which attracted an enthusiastic audience. In addition to her interest in science-fiction, she continued to be an avid Western fan. Finally, in 1965, she completed a book-length Western of her own, *Gunfight at Laramie* (1966). Shortly after this first Western novel was accepted, Hoffman was commissioned by Ace to write a comic Western. It became her second book, *The Legend of Blackjack Sam* (1966), a novel all about "the Notorious Showdown at the O'Shea Corral." The years of writing for the amateur press and her own amusement were now paying off. *The Valdez Horses* (1967) is perhaps her masterpiece. Its emotional impact, aided by a surprise twist in the last line, make this novel difficult to forget. It received the Golden Spur Award from the Western Writers of America. In other novels such as *The Yarborough Brand* (1968) and *West of Cheyenne* (1969), no less than in *The Valdez Horses*, character and motivation are as important as details of the plot. It isn't that Hoffman skimped on action—there are fistfights, gun battles, and chases, but they serve the story rather than being the story's reason for existence. Hoffman refused to be predictable. In common with B. M. Bower before her and P. A. Bechko after, Hoffman tried her hand more than once at comic Westerns, notably in *Wiley's Move* (1973) and *The Truth About The Cannonball Kid* (1975). R. E. Briney in the second edition of the *Encyclopedia of Frontier and Western Fiction* concludes that Hoffman has always had "an enviable command of the writer's craft and the storyteller's art."

WILD RIDERS

Lee Hoffman

First published by Robert Hale, Ltd.

This hardback edition 2003
by Chivers Press
by arrangement with
Golden West Literary Agency

ISBN 0 7540 8214 8

British Library Cataloguing in Publication Data available.

Printed and bound in Great Britain by
BOOKCRAFT, Midsomer Norton, Somerset

TO JO AND DON MEISNER
FOR COFFEE, CAKE AND CONVERSATION

CHAPTER 1

The old oak by the gate was silhouetted against the brilliant fire colors of the sunset sky. A noose dangled from a low limb, swaying slightly.

Topping a rise in the road, Bradenton jerked rein. He rose in the stirrups to stare at the noose and test the wind. It was chill, carrying harsh memories of the winter just past. But the scent he'd caught in it was of warm ashes, still smoldering and dribbling a faint tang of smoke.

The bay horse shuffled restlessly. It was eager to be home again, within the shelter of the barn, nosing into a manger of hay. He had been eager to get home, too. But now there wasn't any barn framed against the sky. No dark shapes of a house and outbuildings rose from the slopes. Only the tall shaft of the stone chimney still stood, pointing upward like an accusing finger.

He understood well enough. The War of the Rebellion had been over for two years, but the fighting in Missouri hadn't ended yet.

"Goddamned jayhawkers," he whispered softly. Then he spat and wiped at his mouth with the back of his hand. *Were they still there, hidden in the brush, waiting . . . ?*

He looked toward the dark line of timber beyond the fields and at the shadowed hollows of the rolling land. There was cover enough for men to hide easily in the dim twilight. And he was well within rifle range of much of that cover.

He told himself they'd be gone now. That noose was left as a warning. When they struck to kill, there wouldn't be any warning—would there?

The bay snuffled, tugging at the bit as he eased rein. With a sudden wild shout, he rammed his spurs at its flanks.

It lunged frantically at the jab. Snorting hard, it raced up the wagon track toward the fence. He bent low over the pommel, screaming like a frenzied devil. And silently cursing the law that denied him a gun.

The bay took the gate in a clean leap, landing into its stride. He wheeled it past the oak, swinging to circle the ashes of the cabin.

There was nothing left but charred wood, fire ruins, and

ashes. The place must have been drenched with coal oil, inside and out, to burn so thoroughly, he thought.

The barn was just as bad. Bright unwinking eyes of embers stared at him from the rubble. Charred and smoldering mounds lying in the ashes had been animals. One lone hen had escaped and was busy pecking at the scattered remnants of his seed corn. She shrieked, scrambling out of the way and clucking curses as he drove the running horse close past her.

He stopped shouting. As he turned back toward the gate, he eased the horse's pace. If there had been ambushers in the brush, that wild charge sure should have drawn fire. He was satisfied that no one was leveling a gun at his back from the shadows.

Halting under the oak, he fingered the noose. It was made of soft cotton rope. Probably his own plow line. He jerked open his clasp knife with his teeth. Standing in the stirrups, he slashed at the rope.

It was too dark to hunt for signs of the men who'd done all this, he thought as he stuffed the noose into a pocket. And it wouldn't do any good anyway. Gigging the horse, he headed back the way he'd come.

It wasn't far to the Potter farm. He paused on the rise overlooking it. The dying light of the sun stretched long shadows behind the house and outbuildings. Nothing stirred. Not a single chicken or hog or hound. But for one window glowing with lamplight, there was no sign of life. The place had an ominously deserted look to it.

Urging the horse into a lope, he started down. As he swung into the yard, he sung out. But he realized he'd already been seen coming. He kept the horse moving fast.

The front windows caught and reflected the setting sun. He couldn't see through, but he could tell one window was slightly open. Just far enough for a gun barrel to be poked out under it. He spotted the dark snout of the gun resting on the sill. It pointed toward him, following him.

As he passed the corner of the house, he jerked the horse to a wheeling halt and sidled it up to the wall. Anyone trying to shoot at him from the windows would be firing at an awkward angle. He hoped nobody was behind the barn with a gun.

Lying low over the horse's neck, ready to slam his spurs into its sides, he hollered, "Sam?"

From inside the house, he heard faint shufflings, then the rusty scraping of a seldom-used lock being forced to work. Unoiled hinges squeaked.

"That you, Brade?" The voice was Sam Potter's.

"Yeah."

The hinges complained again. Footsteps sounded on the planks of the stoop. Potter called, "Lemme see you."

Brade lifted rein and stepped the horse past the edge of the house.

Potter was standing on the stoop with the rifle ready in his hands. He let the muzzle droop. In a voice that wasn't much more than a whisper, he said, "You been up to your place?"

"Yeah."

"They rode past here. I was afraid they might come back. Still afraid of it. Put your horse into the barn. Come on in the kitchen."

Nodding, Brade turned the bay. He found Potter's draft horses and the milk cow in stalls in the barn. The hogs that usually ran free as they pleased were penned too. Even the yard chickens had been run into the barn.

He tied up the bay, hayed it, and closed the door behind him as he headed for the house. Potter opened the kitchen door to him. As he stepped in, the farmer slammed it and twisted the latch, muttering, "Wish I had a decent bar on this."

"Wouldn't do you any good," Brade said. "If they really wanted to get at you, they'd fire the house. It don't do any good penning your stock in the barn either."

The look Potter shot him was cold and accusing. "*You* know all about . . ." He stopped himself.

Tonelessly, Brade finished it for him. "Yeah, I know all about stock-stealing and barn-burning."

The hostility had only flared for a moment. It was gone now, leaving the farmer's face tired and resigned. He mumbled apologetically. But that instant of accusation had been a sharp, unexpected jab, and it still hurt. Brade stood studying the man in front of him.

Potter was lean and long-boned, come of Kentucky mountain stock like himself. The families had been friends back in the hill country before they'd moved west into Missouri. Brade's father and this man had been friends from boyhood. Potters had been like kinfolk to Brade.

"They rode right past here," Potter was saying. "Was four or five of 'em, I think. Maybe that same bunch who robbed Mitchell's bank last fall. I don't know. I seen 'em riding up, but didn't pay no mind. Not till I seen the smoke from over your way. I knew then what they was up to, but wasn't nothing I could do. Nothing. They come back past riding hard, and my hound took out after them. He ain't come home. I expect he won't never come home. I'm a peaceable man, Brade. There wasn't nothing I could do."

"No, I reckon not."

Mrs. Potter came through the doorway. Brushing a loose strand of hair back from her forehead, she tried to give him a bright smile. But worry marred her face.

"Evening, Brade," she said. "You look tired. Set, and I'll fetch you something to eat."

"Obliged." He pulled a chair out from the table and settled into it. As he stretched out his legs, he looked at his boots.

Polished boots, his good suit, a clean shirt with a soft tie at the collar, and his black felt hat that was still too new to wear for working in—remembering the hat, he pulled it off and set it down. He'd slicked up for the trip into Lexington as if he'd been going to Sunday meeting. Done himself up to look respectable and rode in to pay his taxes, all nice and peaceable and law-abiding.

That was the hell of it, he thought. Man paid a tax on his property and came home to find it all burnt off. The law denied him a gun to protect his belongings himself. But he knew damn well that for *him* to go complaining to the law would do about as much good as hollering his troubles down a rain barrel.

Potter was still standing there holding the rifle as if he wasn't at all sure what he ought to do now. Eyeing it, Brade muttered, "I got to get hold of a gun."

Mrs. Potter turned to face him. "Caudell Prescott Bradenton! You gave the gov'ment your parole! What would your poor dead folks say if they could hear you talk of breaking your solemn oath?"

"They worked themselves to death building that farm. Twice!" he answered. "What do you think they'd say to having it burnt off again? Every damn plank and beam and stick turned to ashes. The stock slaughtered and the seed scattered."

She hesitated. "An oath is an oath. You gave your word, and the provost marshal gave you a paper. You promised the United States of America you wouldn't take up a gun again."

"*They* promised *me* I could come home and live peaceful. They promised me the war was over and I could take up planting without more trouble. What does this look like?" He jerked the noose out of his pocket and tossed it on the table. She jumped as if it was a snake he'd slung down in front of her.

Potter stared at it. "Where'd you get that?"

"It was hanging in my yard, waiting for me."

The moment of silence drew out long, almost to snapping. Then the woman sighed. "Well, I don't know what's right anymore. But you gave them your *word,* Brade."

"I know." He didn't look at her as he answered her. "I don't like going against it. But I don't like having my place burnt to the ground. And I wouldn't like being lynched either."

"But—"

"Ma, you hush up," Potter interrupted. "This is *men's* business."

She sighed again. Shrugging, she turned to poke up the fire and set a skillet on the stove.

Potter asked, "What about going to the law?"

"*Bluebelly* law?"

He rubbed a hand along the rifle. Then he set it against the wall. Pulling out a chair, he seated himself across the table from Brade. Soft-voiced, he said, "We're thinking of leaving. Going further west. Take up a place in the new lands. Why don't you come along with us, Brade?"

"No."

"If you stay here, you're gonna find trouble."

"I was born and raised here. I've fought and killed and been outlawed and chased and nigh to got myself killed for this land. I'm not going to quit it now and walk off just on account of some damned jayhawkers. Not going to let them have my land without . . ." For an instant, he hesitated. He finished in the same tone, "A fight."

His eyes were on the closed door into the hallway. Wordlessly, Potter watched him rise and start silently toward it.

Brade picked up the rifle in one hand as he reached for the doorknob with the other. He stepped back, jerking up the gun as he slammed open the door.

The girl let out a thin, startled squeal.

She was small and slender, the top of her head coming about even with his chin. For an instant, her upturned face was drained of color. Then bright spots of red began to appear on her cheeks.

"Amy!" her mother sputtered in mixed anger and relief.

"What the devil do you think you're doing?" Brade grunted, glaring at her.

"I heard voices," she said plaintively. The eyes that seemed sometimes brown and sometimes green gazed wide into his. The straw-colored lashes flickered. And the guilty fear that had been in her eyes disappeared. She smiled at him.

"You were listening at the door, weren't you?" Mrs. Potter snapped at her.

"Ought to have your bottom tanned," Brade said.

The color brightened on her cheeks. Her smile turned to an embarrassed scowl.

"You were told to stay upstairs." Potter started to his feet.

"But, Pa, I thought—"

"I don't care what you thought. You do what you're *told.*"

"But it's just Brade. Can't I visit a while?"

"No!"

"Pa—"

"No!"

She looked to Brade again. Her teeth sunk lightly into her lower lip, and her moist eyes pleaded silently for him to back her up.

He glared at her a moment, then turned away and set down the rifle.

Her heels made hard clacking sounds on the bare planks as she stomped off, back to her exile upstairs.

"She know what happened at my place?" he asked Potter when she was gone.

"She knows, but she don't hardly understand these things. The border troubles been going on since she was a baby. She's heard plenty about burning and raiding and killing, but she's never known it to be any other way. Sometimes she acts like she thinks it's all some kind of game."

He nodded, remembering. In the beginning, it had been like a game to him, too. The wild riding, the fighting, the destruction had all been one grand game of hare and hounds. Back then, he'd looked at burning homes as if they were autumn bonfires.

Memories were like dream images in his mind. A city in flames, the terrified voices, the screaming and shooting, the hammering hooves—somebody had made a song about it later. *All routing and shouting and giving the yell, like so many demons just raised up from hell, the boys they were drunken with powder and wine, and came to burn Lawrence just over the line . . .*

After a time, it had stopped being like a game at all.

"We've got to take her away from here," Potter said suddenly from the depths of his own thoughts.

Brade gave a shake of his head, trying to clear away the cobwebs of memory. He asked, "You just going to walk off and leave your land? Leave everything you've built here?"

"I got a chance to sell it. Was a man around just a day or two ago, made me an offer. Nothing like what the place is worth, but enough to stake us. We got to take Amy away from here."

"But you held out all through the war . . ."

"All through the war I kept thinking pretty soon it would be over. I wasn't much for politics, and I never owned a slave. Never even thought of owning one. Didn't give a damn which side won, long as someday it ended. But now it's beginning to look like it ain't *ever* going to end around here. I'm sick of war!"

"You weren't ever attacked," Brade said.

Potter snorted, "Wasn't I? Bushwackers and jayhawkers both! Sure, they never burnt me out, but over and over I had stock confiscated and crops foraged. The Federals and Secesh just helped themselves. *You,* Brade! You and them friends of yours, you trompled through my cornfields more'n once when you holed up in the woods back yonder. You helped yourselves to my truck and my chickens and hogs . . ."

Brade eyed him sideways. "I thought you were glad to help out our cause."

"I didn't give a damn about your *cause.* But with all the firearms you and your friends carried, I wasn't gonna speak up to complain how you were stealing from me."

Mrs. Potter put in, "I wouldn't have spoke up to that Captain Bill Anderson even if he never had a gun on him. Just the look of that man's eyes would take the voice right out of me. You were all fierce, mean-looking boys, Caudell Prescott Bradenton."

He shook his head slowly in uncertain surprise. "I knew you didn't talk about your feelings, but I always thought you favored us. Thought you helped us because you *wanted* to."

"You always thought whatever you wanted to think," she answered. She brought the skillet to the table and ladled slices of ham and fried corn mush onto the plate in front of him. "You really think I *liked* having my little girl-child run off up to the woods to visit your camp and all those wild boys you rode with?"

"You never said nothing at all about it," he protested.

"Your folks were good friends and good neighbors while they were alive. We knew you for a decent boy before you took up with the bushwackers, and we prayed to the Lord that you'd look out for Amy. But we were awful scared."

"We're peaceable folk," Potter said. "You've been a good neighbor yourself, since you come home and settled. Couldn't see no need to trouble you by complaining of what had been and was over. But now it looks like it ain't over."

His wife spoke again. "You've got a smell of smoke and ashes about you tonight, Brade. It's the smell of trouble. All of west Missouri is stinking of trouble. Our little girl's not a baby-child anymore. She's turning ripe into a woman. We can't keep her here any longer. Not with the jayhawkers prowling around here. It isn't anything against *you,* Brade. It's the way things are. You understand that, don't you?"

He nodded, still surprised that he could have been friends with these folk so long without knowing about this part of their feelings. Now he began to wonder whether they were asking him to understand because of their friendship or because they were still afraid of him.

She looked at him thoughtfully. "Why don't you do like Pa says, Brade? Why don't you come along with us?"

"I haven't got any reason to run," he said. "I don't have a family here that could get hurt. And I ain't scared."

"You should be. If you go pick up a gun and break your parole, you'll get proscribed. You'll be back in the bush again, but not with any Quantrill's Irregulars this time. You'll be alone, Brade. If the jayhawkers don't get you, the law will."

"No, ma'am." He nudged at the noose still laying on the table. "Leastways, not until I've got a few of them. Nobody's going to run me off by waving a rope at me. That's the second house the jayhawkers have burnt off that land. Somebody's going to pay for that."

She didn't try arguing back. She just stood there gazing at him with a deep sadness in her eyes.

He looked toward Potter, thinking maybe a man would understand better than a woman. Matters of pride and honor were man's business. But Potter turned away from taking sides.

Silently, Brade busied himself with the food. As he ate, he considered one of the things Potter had said earlier. He asked, "This feller who offered to buy your place, was he one of our people or a Unionist?"

"Wasn't anybody from around these parts," Potter said. "Called himself Orin Coleman."

The name meant nothing to Brade.

Hopefully, Mrs. Potter suggested, "He might buy your land too, Brade. He was asking about it. Seemed real interested. It'd give you a stake to start up fresh somewhere else where names like *bushwacker* won't mean so much. I know Amy'd be awful glad if you came with us."

Brade didn't answer her. He spoke to Potter, thinking it out as he talked. "Sam, you know I'm not the only ex-guerilla who's been burnt out and threatened with worse since we surrendered."

Of the men who'd been his own friends, one was dead, lynched by masked men wearing the kind of red leggings that had been the uniform with Jennison's men. One had only managed to escape raiding vigilantes by hiding under the seat in his outhouse. Another had been jumped and beaten almost to death out on the road in broad daylight.

"The Kansans claim they're only getting even with the bushwackers for the things we done to them during the war," he continued. "But I'm starting to wonder if that's the whole of it."

"What?" Potter asked.

"More'n a few fellers have sold out and moved to get their families away from trouble. Suppose that was just what somebody had in mind."

"I don't follow you."

"I'm asking myself if I was burnt out *just* because I rode with Quantrill and Todd. The jayhawkers know I got damn little recourse under the terms I surrendered to. Suppose somebody got the idea I could be run off real easy without I'd pick up a gun and fight back?"

"You mean they burnt you out just to get your land away from you?" Mrs. Potter said.

"That's what I'm wondering."

Potter's forehead creased in a deep, thoughtful frown. "You think it was this same man who offered to buy my land?"

"I can't say. But you tell me, Sam, would you be willing to sell and pull out now if it hadn't been for the raid on my place?"

He shook his head. "Damned if I'm so sure now that I want to sell at all. It's one thing to get edged off your land by troubles. Another thing altogether to be *tricked* off it."

"Well, I'm not being edged or tricked either one," Brade said. He poked his fork at a ring of ham bone lying on the plate in front of him. "Hell or high water, I'm not going to be run out. As far as I'm concerned, their damn amnesty is ashes along with my buildings. I'll get hold of a gun—"

"They'll catch you, Brade," Mrs. Potter interrupted. "They'll kill you."

"Maybe," he muttered, studying on the ham bone as if it held some deep interest for him. "In the end, it might be they'll get my land. But I swear they won't be getting it *cheap*."

CHAPTER 2

Something woke Brade suddenly. He lay motionless in the loft, listening for any sound that didn't belong. The hay was stiff and crackly, with a dead smell to it. Old, dry hay. The barn walls and the loft floor under him were old and dry, too. Dry as tinder.

His hand felt god-awful empty without a gun in it.

Thin dusty shafts of sunlight angled into the barn through knotholes and cracks between the planks. They reflected a dim glow around them. Propping himself on his elbows, he squirmed forward and gazed at the barn door. He didn't think it was a jayhawker prowling outside. But something was sure messing around near the door.

The crack of light along it widened slightly, a part blocked by shadow. It hesitated, then grew again.

He grinned as he recognized the figure silhouetted against the dawn. Amy was standing there with a pail in her hand, surveying the dusky barn. He didn't think there was light enough for her to see him in the loft. She'd know he'd slept the night there though.

She slipped cautiously through the narrow opening. Taking careful, quiet steps, she moved out of his sight, blocked by the loft floor. He wriggled himself closer to the edge, silently as a snake, and peered over at her. She set down the bucket by the cow's stall, then turned to head toward the ladder on tiptoe.

He grabbed the edge of the floor and rolled, swinging himself over. For a moment he hung dangling by his fingertips, facing her.

It was a piece of show-off for her, but what the hell, he thought. Amy had a way of bringing out the kid-foolishness in him. He figured as long as he knew what he was doing and why, there was no harm in it. No harm in kidding around a bit for the little girl on the farm next door.

She squeaked with surprise. For an instant, her face paled, and her eyes gaped wide.

Maybe it had been the wrong time to pull a prank like that, he thought as he let go. Dropping to the ground, he started to apologize for giving her such a start.

"Oh, goodness, Brade!" she moaned with a deep sigh, "You *scared* me!" She was trying hard to look solemn and indignant, but she was having trouble keeping back a grin.

He held off the apology. She didn't need it, and she didn't really deserve it. Instead, he said, "Serves you right for trying to sneak up on me. You ought to know better than that."

"I wasn't trying to sneak up. I just didn't want to waken you."

He snorted through his nose. That was a lie, and he knew it. She probably realized that. It was just a game. But not *all* of it.

Completely serious, he said, "You're lucky I don't have a

gun. The way you go around listening at doors and creeping up on people, someday you're going to get yourself hurt."

"I didn't want to waken you," she repeated, pouting. Her eyes dared him to condemn her for it.

He did. Keeping his face straight and stern, he said, "Like hell. You figured you could catch me asleep and show me up. If you ever managed that, you'd never stop ragging me about it."

"Oh, *you!*" she snapped, shaking her head. "Lieutenant Caudell Prescott Bradenton, the big know-it-all soldier! Commissioned in the field by old Bill Quantrill himself. And *who* commissioned Mister Quantrill, you tell me that?"

"Gideon Thompson and Jefferson Davis. What's that got to do with anything?"

"You think just because he *called* you an officer and a gentleman you know everything, don't you?"

"No. I learned it all the hard way." He gave her a condescending grin.

She wheeled away from him, but not before he could see the color rising in her cheeks. Stomping over to the cow stall, she picked up her pail.

He followed, grinning at the way she jerked out the milking stool and flung the bucket into place. Folding his arms on the Ayeshire's rump, he leaned over to watch.

She set into milking with a fury that shocked the old cow into a deep low of protest.

Brade laughed out loud.

For a moment, Amy hung onto her embarrassed anger. But then she let it slide away and looked up at him, laughing herself. "Someday I'll catch you, Caudell Prescott Bradenton!"

He wondered why womenfolk were so fond of throwing a man's whole christened name at him that way, like it was a string of cuss words. Nobody ever hung the Caudell Prescott part onto him except a woman when she was trying to get the best of him.

She stopped laughing. Her face went soft and serious. In a whispery voice, she said, "I won't ever get the chance, Brade. We're going away."

"Your folks told me."

"Pa asked you to come with us, didn't he?"

He nodded slightly, wondering if she'd heard that by listening at the door.

"Please come!"

"No. I got business around here."

"In the bush?"

He nodded again. He had a feeling she'd already known

his answer. Had she heard everything he and her father had talked over last night?

She gazed at him in that deep, wide-eyed, pleading way she'd used on him since she was just big enough to run around without falling on her face. Back then, she'd used it to get him to amuse her with tricks like walking the top fence rails or turning tumblesalts or because she wanted to be lifted up to ride the plow horse. Back then, it had been fun having her nag at him to show off, then basking in her admiration. But lately, he'd begun to get an uncomfortable feeling when she looked at him that way. And her downright admiration gave him a damn warm sense of discomfort.

She was pleading silently with him now to give up on Missouri and head west along with her family. She begged him and added something of accusation, as if he'd be wronging her by refusing.

"Brade," she said slowly.

From the tone of her voice, he knew there was more to come, and he knew what it would be. He wished to hell he could stop her of it. He was tempted to clamp a hand over her mouth and shove the words back down her throat.

"Brade, I love you."

"Dammit, Amy!" he began. He wasn't sure what to say. Closing his mouth, he refused to meet her eyes.

That had been different once, too. Some five or six years ago, when she was a scrawny-legged kid with knobby knees she showed the world when she ran across the fields, he'd been delighted to have her fling her arms around his neck and shout, "I love you!"

It had been like a kid sister's adoration then. But now, she was old enough to know what it could mean—too damned old to go around saying it all the time. And still too young to—hell, she was just a *little girl*. She was the Potter kid from the next farm. He didn't want to think the kind of thoughts about her that she'd begun to put into his mind. Not about *Amy!*

Firmly, he said, "I don't love you. Not the way you think you mean. You know that."

She gave a sigh, like someone who'd been trying to explain something to a stubborn child and had gotten nowhere with it.

That annoyed him, too—that motherly way she'd begun to take with him at times. He was more than half again her age. She had no business acting like a mother toward him. Or like a grown woman. She was just a *little girl*.

When he didn't say anything more, she got herself very busy with the cow. He turned to feeding the stock. By the time he was done, she had finished milking and was putting up the stool. Wordlessly, he took the pail and started for the door. She hurried to catch up and keep pace with his long stride.

"You're a mule!" she snapped suddenly.

He grinned at her scolding tone. He didn't like it—but yet he did. That was one of the most annoying things about her —the feelings she stirred in him were always so mixed. He could be angry and disgusted with her, but fondly amused, even pleased, at the same time.

It would be a relief to have her move away, he told himself. But it'd be kind of lonesome, too.

Breakfast in the kitchen was strange. The restraint and tension he could sense in the Potters had him feeling like an intruder. They'd claimed that they didn't hold him to blame for their troubles, but he kept wondering if that wasn't the thought in their minds.

Since she'd come into the house, Amy had gotten quiet and withdrawn, too. She hardly spoke to him, and then it was to make some taunt about him being bonded to a piece of land like a slave. She didn't seem able to understand that it wasn't the land but a matter of pride. She couldn't really know how much of his self-respect he'd given up by surrendering to the terms the Bluebellies had imposed to the Missouri bushwackers. He couldn't let the last of it be torn away from him by fire and threats. He *couldn't* let himself be run off. A man was better off honorably dead than alive but shamed in his own eyes.

When they were finished eating, Potter got to his feet in a slow, thoughtful way. Frowning, he gave a shake of his head, like he'd reached a conclusion he wasn't sure about.

"One day back in the war, I found a dead boy out in the cornfield. All shot up. Couldn't tell was he a jayhawker or one of your bunch," he said as he hunkered stiffly to dig into the food safe. "Nothing on him to say who he was or where he come from. Nothing but this."

He pulled out a rag-wrapped parcel and handed it to Brade. "Might be you ought to have it."

Brade peeled back the cloth. It was a Colt Patent revolver, the octagonal-barreled Navy caliber. The brass was dull, the walnut butt smooth-worn and almost black with using. The chambers were empty, the nipples bare. It looked like it had been carefully cleaned and stored away. But from the condition of the nipples and the rest, it had been well used before that.

As it settled into his hand, he felt a sudden strength and

confidence. Easing back the hammer, he tried the trigger spring and judged the action to be in good working order.

"I'm obliged," he said.

Potter pulled another bundle out of the safe. "There's a few caps and balls. And I got powder you can take from."

He repeated his thanks as Potter handed him the powder flask.

"Wasn't nothing I could do for the boy but bury him decent. Up yonder on the edge of the woods," Potter continued. "I hope he was one of your people, Brade. I mean, I hope it's not *his* that you'll be taking that pistol against."

Amy stared at Brade's hands as he capped off the nipples, eased the hammer down onto a safety peg, and thrust the gun into his waistband. He could feel the unhappiness in her gaze. He shoved the gun toward his hip and tugged the skirt of his coat over to cover it.

Mrs. Potter said quietly, "Don't let them catch you, Brade."

"No, ma'am, I won't."

"You fool!" Amy snapped, her voice high and thin. She turned, mumbling under her breath, and dashed out of the room.

He looked at the door she slammed behind her, wishing there'd been some way to make her understand.

Potter broke the harsh silence. "Ma, you fetch up and get yourself and Amy ready. I want you both to come along with me to town."

As she left the room, Brade turned to Potter. "You're going in to see that land-buyer?"

He nodded. "I want to get this done and over with."

"I'd like to go with you."

His eyes narrowed warily. He asked Brade, "You mean to kill him?"

"I'm not planning to walk up and put a ball into his gut, if that's what you're worried about. I want to see him and talk to him. If he is the one who burnt me out, he'll be looking for me to come trying to sell my land. I want to see what kind of reaction I get from him."

"All right," Potter muttered, still hesitant. "I'll take you to him. Only, promise me, Brade. You've got to promise you'll let me finish my business and get clear before you—before the trouble starts. I've got to take care of my womenfolk."

"Sure, Sam. I'm not planning to do anything against him till I'm certain he's the one I'm after."

"Won't hurt you none to take your time."

He nodded, hoping Potter was right. He hoped to hell he

didn't catch a jayhawker's bullet in the back before he could get his own business with the land-buyer finished.

Lexington, Missouri, was a town of mixed sympathies. Back in 'sixty-one, when Sterling Price's troops had won the battle of the Hemp Bales, a lot of the folk around had claimed to be Secesh. Quite a few of them still stood by their word. But as county seat, the town had more than its share of Unionists and Bluebellies around.

Brade was uncomfortably aware of the revolver tucked into the waistband of his britches now. Just having that was a breach of his parole. But it was well hidden under his coat, and nobody had any reason to look at him suspiciously. Not yet.

As he followed Potter into the hotel, he could feel the dull aching in his right thigh. That ache was as much a part of him as the scar that lay over it. He'd grown so accustomed to it that he rarely noticed or thought about it. But as he waited, he felt it and remembered the pain of the fresh wound.

Potter exchanged words with the man at the desk, then came back to tell Brade, "He's gone. Left on the eastbound coach. Didn't leave no address but St. Louis. Nothing else."

Brade frowned. It didn't make sense. Not if he'd been right in what he'd thought about the land-buyer. And he wanted desperately to be right.

The man had been real—an individual with a name—Orin Coleman. He'd been a person who could be caught up with. But if he were the one behind the burning and the threat, he should be waiting here now, looking to pick up the land cheap. Only, he wasn't here.

The face Brade had hoped for was gone. The raiders might have been Kansas men, come from the other side of the state line and gone back again. Or they could have been Missouri charcoals, even Lafayette County people—his own neighbors. More than a few folk held the bushwackers to blame for all the troubles that had come onto Missouri in the past years. If Coleman wasn't the man behind the raid on his farm, Brade was left with only nameless, faceless phantoms to chase.

Taking leave of Potter, he headed down the street. A vaguely uneasy, spied-on feeling followed him. As he passed the group of men lounging in front of the bank, he nodded casually to the ones he knew. Without trying, he saw their faces vividly. He saw the buildings around him as sharply as if he looked through a strong pair of field glasses. He felt the warmth and light of the sun on his shoulders. He heard the rattle of wagons, hooves clomping, people conversing. It was the sensitivity of the hunted—the same instinct that had apprehension crawling like flies along his spine.

He wasn't one with the people who ambled along the walk. He felt singled out, watched by someone with a definite purpose. He was being followed. By the time he'd reached the corner beyond the barbershop, he was certain of it.

Wheeling abruptly, he turned the corner. There was no one on the road ahead. He stretched his stride into a near run, turning again at the back of the corner building. Ducking into its shadow, he stopped dead.

It was a still, quiet morning. The murmur of the town was soft—a mixture of voices, of wagons and animals, a slammed door, a muffled steady clatter of a printing press—a dull gray smear of sounds. The sudden red slash of footsteps on gravel cut across it. Someone had turned onto the side street in a hurry.

The steps paused.

A man stood there looking up the road, Brade thought. A man who wondered what had become of his quarry.

He felt his fingers flex, longing to wrap around the butt of the revolver. He held back from it, telling himself it wasn't time yet to show his fangs.

Gravel crunched under a bootsole. The hunter walked slowly and cautiously now, with a sound of uncertainty.

Brade waited, judging the man's position from the steps that came closer, hesitated, then came on. Suddenly, he stepped out into the road, to face the man.

He hadn't been mistaken. He recognized the hunter.

Ben Holgram was one of the bunch who'd ridden under Bill Anderson's command. Startled, he tottered in midstride, staring at Brade. A corner of his mouth twitched slightly. Then he smiled, trying to look surprised. "Hell, if it ain't Lieutenant Bradenton! How the devil've you been?"

Brade gave him no return greeting. Instead, he said coldly, "You got a reason for stalking me?"

"Didn't mean no harm by it. Wanted to talk to you someplace quiet. Not out there where all the Bluebellies could see us together."

"It's pretty quiet here."

He looked past Brade at the empty road, as if he expected to see the dust clouds of an oncoming column of horsemen. Then he shot a glance over his shoulder. Whatever secret he was carrying, it seemed to weigh heavily on him. Finally, in a near whisper, he said, "I hear there was some trouble down your way yesterday."

Brade nodded slightly, noncommitally, though there was a

sudden taste of excitement in the back of his mouth. Did Holgram know something about that jayhawk raid?

"Heard your place burnt."

"Yeah."

Holgram looked as though he'd hoped for more response than that. He asked, "You been in to complain to the law about it."

"No."

"Going to complain to them?" His voice had a wedge to it like a prybar.

Brade bit back the urge to start asking his own questions. He wanted to let Holgram lay out **his** whole hand first. But impatience was burning in his gut. Keeping his face blank, he said blandly, "Think I should?"

"Hell!" Holgram grunted in frustration. Impatience was burning in him, too. He almost squirmed with the need to know something of Brade's thoughts before he spilled out anything else. His eyes pleaded with Brade, begging for an answer.

Brade wasn't at all sure what the question might be. He snapped, "Whatever you're selling, either show me your goods or peddle your pack somewhere else."

"Hell!" Holgram repeated. He drew a breath, collecting himself, and set in again. "You ain't exactly happy with the way things are in Missouri these days, are you, Brade?"

The answer to that should have been obvious. "I ain't been happy with the way things been in Missouri for the past eight or ten years. Why?"

The blunt-edged question seemed to kick some of the wind out of Holgram. He poised as if he were balanced on a high, precarious perch. "I *can* trust you, can't I?"

"At what?"

"You wouldn't of been picked if I couldn't trust you," he said to reassure himself. "You'll give me your word you won't talk about it to nobody else?"

"Talk about what?" Brade felt his voice grind through the tightness of his throat. The impatience swirled up from his gut, through his shoulders and arms, into his fingertips. His hands begged to snatch at Holgram's neck and choke the damned slow-coming answers out of him. He held them back from it.

"Just promise me you won't tell," Holgram said.

"All right. You got my word."

"What I want to know, Brade, is would you be willing to do some more fighting to get the government of this state back into the hands of good Missouri folk like us?"

"Huh?"

"Would you fight to get the vote back for the Rebs?" Holgram went on, sounding like he was reciting. "To get back your rights as a citizen of the state and the nation?"

Warily, Brade asked, "You talking about fighting with a gun?"

"Don't try telling me you ain't got a pistol under your coat," Holgram protested. "You've already broke your parole, ain't you? You got good reason for it. You got *good* reason for coming in with the rest of us!"

"What the hell are you talking about?"

"A kind of work like you've done before. Fighting to get what's rightfully yours."

Brade eyed him, incredulous at the thought that had begun to grow in his mind. He spoke it out. "You ain't trying to raise an army and start the war again?"

"You might say that," Holgram grinned.

"You recall what happened to us in the last war we started?"

"It ain't exactly the same." He squirmed under Brade's scrutiny. Almost plaintively, he said, "I can't tell you all about it yet. I'm just supposed to see would you be interested. We'd sure like to have you in with us."

"Who's this *we?"*

"Mostly it's Bob Alan Logan. You 'member Bob Alan? Had a bunch of his own during the war. Used to team up with Anderson now and then for an action after Anderson busted up with Quantrill. 'Member the raid on Centralia?"

"Yeah," Brade muttered. He remembered a damn lot of things. Some of them still gave him an ugly queasiness in his stomach. He focused on his recollection of Bob Alan Logan.

The man had paired up fine with Bloody Bill Anderson. They'd had a lot in common, though Logan was quieter and cooler in battle. He'd seemed to have the makings of a good officer, though he never kept a full company. He'd had a small hand-picked bunch riding with him, and mostly they worked alone. Brade had a notion they'd preferred robbing coaches and stealing horses to outright warfare. A lot of the Irregulars had been more bandit than soldier. As he recalled him, Logan was a shrewd man. Far too clever to have wild ideas about starting the war over.

"He's heading things up," Holgram was saying. "He was here himself, meaning to see you. But he got a telegraph message yesterday and had to leave out last night. Left me here to talk to you. If you're interested, I'm supposed to bring you to meet with him."

"I got to know more of what you're talking about before I'll know if I'm interested." It had the sound of midnight business, Brade thought. The kind that was conducted with guns. His first impulse was to stay away from it and out of trouble. But the time for staying out of trouble was past.

"I can't tell you no more, only it's to get back our rights and get the charcoals out of Jefferson City," Holgram said. "I can tell you that much. Logan'll explain all the rest. You're with us, ain't you, Brade?"

It could have to do with striking back at the jayhawkers, too, Brade thought. If he couldn't locate the same men who'd burnt his place, he'd settle for revenging himself against others of the same cut. He answered, "I reckon it won't do me any harm to talk to him."

Holgram's face broadened into a relieved grin. "Be real good to have you with us. You know, Bill Anderson thought right much of you. I recall as how he said he'd like to get you away from Todd's command into his. Said you was a damn fine soldier. That's just what we need."

Brade felt a mingling of pride and embarrassment at the praise. And a hell of a curiosity about this crusade for Missouri that wasn't exactly a war but needed good soldiers.

CHAPTER 3

Holgram led Brade into Benton County, where the rolling plain was left behind and the hills began to grow into mountains. The place was a farm tucked up in the lee of a bluff, surrounded all around by woodlands, and a long ways from anywhere.

At the house, Holgram gave a holler. A man stepped out, nodding in welcome, and told them when they'd turned out their mounts to come on into the kitchen.

There was a good-sized pen behind the barn with a bunch of horses already in it. Drawing rein, Brade slid down off the bay, glad to unkink his legs. They were stiff, and his thigh ached. He was limping slightly as he moved to tend the horse.

"You haven't met Tom Dunkle before?" Holgram asked him.

"Think I've seen him, but can't place him. One of Anderson's men?"

"One of Logan's. Lieutenant to him. This is Dunkle's place. Damn fine hideout."

It looked to be, Brade thought as he followed Holgram toward the house. But just who would Logan's men be hiding from—jayhawkers and local Missouri law, or maybe the whole United States Army? What the hell was this scheme anyway?

There were a dozen or more men in the kitchen, some in the bluff game at the table, some just watching. Brade scanned their faces. Most of them were vaguely familiar, mostly bushwackers. One was a friend—Abel Collis. He nodded. Collis gave him a quick grin in reply, then returned his attention to his cards.

He asked Holgram, "Where's Logan?"

Turning to Dunkle, Holgram said, "Hey, ain't Logan here yet?"

"Tomorrow," Dunkle grunted without looking up from the game. "Next day at the latest."

That was a disappointment. Impatience galled at Brade. And he had a feeling he wasn't the only one here who didn't know what was going on. Most of the men seemed uncomfortably aware of themselves and uncertain of the others. There was a cocked trigger feel to the air.

He watched the game for a while, but it didn't hold his interest. Eventually, he drifted outside.

It looked like it had been a good farm once, but it had been ignored and was falling into ruin. The house needed repairs on the roof and rain gutters. The barn and outbuildings needed to be rebuilt completely. A sluice brought water down from a stream on the bluff, feeding into a ditch across the yard, but the ditch needed to be dug out again. The water overflowed it in places, making thick mud.

Upslope, the soil ran to gravelly clay, but in the bottoms it was rich and black. Nigh begging for a plow to be put to it. The weeds thrived in the fields.

Leaning on a rail of the horse pen, Brade thought as how he'd a lot sooner be putting the bay into a collar for plowing than under a saddle for fighting. But somebody had declared that the war in Missouri wasn't done yet. So somebody had to fight back. Again he wondered what it was Logan had planned that needed good soldiers.

He heard the kitchen door creak open and shut again. Footsteps sounded on the packed earth. The fence rail yielded slightly as Abel Collis leaned on it at his side.

After a long moment, Collis said, "Which one's yours? The bay or the roan?"

"Bay. Roan belongs to Holgram."

"Bay's a good looking horse. You always did have a good eye for a horse."

Brade grinned. He'd had a reputation as one of the handiest horse thieves in Todd's command. He'd taken pride in it.

"'Member that black he-horse we set out to confiscate once in Cass County?" he said.

"The one that tried to kick your head in?"

"Yeah. Seems I recall he got away with your saddle and all your gear on his back."

Collis chuckled softly. "Yeah."

"Seems to me it snowed that night."

"And we both nigh froze to death lying out in the bush with nothing but that raggedy blanket of yours between us."

Brade nodded, gazing at the horses in the pen. It was strange that something as ugly as the war had been could have left memories that he recalled fondly. That sure hadn't been his idea of fun while it was happening. But now he enjoyed the recollection. And it was damn good to see Collis again.

He said, "Coll, what the hell we getting into here?"

"Don't you know either?"

"No. I figure it ain't gonna be anything exactly lawful though."

"Sure don't sound that way," Collis agreed. "I thought you had a place you were going home to. Thought you were going to settle down and farm."

"So did I. But somebody burnt me out a few days ago."

"You too?" Collis straightened up and looked at him. "They hit me a few weeks ago. While me and the family were in to meeting. Must of used coal oil all over everything. Wasn't a whole stick left. I tried talking to the sheriff about it, and he laughed in my face. Told me it was what I deserved."

Brade nodded. "I didn't bother with going to the law. They know me, and I know them."

"There ain't no law left in Missouri that'll protect an ex-Reb."

Thoughtfully, he asked, "Coll, had there been anybody around looking to buy your land before it happened?"

"No, nothing like that."

Well, that was another blow against his notion about that land-buyer being behind the raids, Brade thought. It didn't look like he'd ever find out exactly who'd burnt his farm.

Curious, he asked, "How'd you happen onto this business with Logan?"

"*He* come to *me*. Week or so after the fire. I'd took the missus and younguns to stay with kin and went back to build up again. Logan showed and asked me would I like to hit back at them as done it."

"He knows who they are?"

Collis shook his head. "No, but he knows as well as I do that it was either jayhawkers or Missouri turncoats. He said if I throwed in with him, I'd get a chance to even things up and be helping get the charcoal radicals out of control of this state."

"He didn't mention how he intends to do it, though?"

"He said he wants to get us all together 'fore he does his talking. I'm purely faunching to find out what he's up to."

"Yeah," Brade sighed. There sure wasn't anything to do but wait. He glanced at the horses again. "One of them yours?"

"That pie-faced sorrel. Ornery little bitch, but she's fast as the devil."

"Match you."

"That poor crow-bait of yours against my little mare!" Collis scowled up, making his voice indignant. "My mare's saucy as hell!"

"Might be, but she ain't got the length of leg. I could give you a start though. Say ten yards."

"You're headsprung! I got a silver Yankee dollar that says my mare can start your bay even and be a length ahead by . . ." He looked toward the road and pointed, "From the front of the house to that twisted-up white oak yonder."

Brade studied on the mare. She was smallish and compact. From the depth of her barrel and the set of her rump, he judged her for a sprinter. He suggested, "Front of the house to the oak and back."

"I just made a dollar," Collis grinned confidently.

The prospect of a horse race broke up the bluff game in the kitchen. The men crowded out in front of the house, bargaining wagers among themselves as Brade and Collis saddled up.

When he settled on the bay, Brade realized he should have put the race off till morning. The horse had done a good day's work since breakfast. It still had ginger, but it lacked the fine edge he'd need for racing. Too late to change things now though. Glancing at the men who watched him, he knew he couldn't suggest it in front of them. It would seem too much like backing down. That would hurt his pride worse than losing.

Sometimes a man got himself into a thing there just wasn't any way out of, he thought as he nudged the bay up to the score. Nothing to do but go through with it and keep his head up when he lost.

The bay flung itself forward at the blast of the starting

gun. It knew racing and didn't need the jab of Brade's spurs against its flanks. It stretched eagerly into the match.

But the mare was a quick little animal. She was half a length ahead in the first few strides. The bay managed to close on her until they were side by side at the oak. She could wheel sharper though. She gained back her lead in the turn.

Bent low over the pommel, Brade drove the bay. But he could feel it tiring. Silently, he cursed the horse—and himself. He couldn't exactly afford to throw away a dollar on a bad bet. But the mare's outstretched muzzle was well ahead of the bay's when they crossed the score again.

Laughing, Collis slid out of the saddle and patted the sorrel's neck. He looked up at Brade. "Told you she was the devil's little sister!"

Swinging down off the bay, Brade dug a hand into a pocket. He fished out coin and script.

"I don't take shinplasters," Collis said.

"Nobody does." Brade shoved aside the paper. He sorted ninety cents worth of coin out of the stuff in his hand and held it toward Collis. "I owe you ten cents. And I'll match you again when my horse is rested up decent."

"You got a match."

Their race had given the men ideas. Already a couple of others were saddling up to run their horses. The rest were making more bets.

While they watched, Collis helped Brade put names to most of their faces. Ron Goforth, Lige Gargan, and Adolph Rll were farmers from the Burnt-Out District. Charleston Bees and Bill Archer were teamsters, both big husky men who looked like they could wrassle oxen barehanded. Jake and Littleton Spring were strangers, brothers from up around Keytesville. They were the only ones of the bunch who hadn't ridden with the bushwackers. Jake had been a regular soldier under Sterling Price. Little was too young to have soldiered. He wasn't more than seventeen or eighteen now, Brade figured. He looked like an eager, swaggering kid who thought he'd missed out on a lot of fun during the war. Seemed determined to make up for it in the action to come. He had two big Army caliber Remington revolvers stuck into the wide belt he wore, and a Bowie knife in a sheath hung off it.

A wild kid like that could cause trouble, Brade thought as he watched the way the boy moved and laughed and made reckless bets. Then it occurred to him that he'd probably been a lot the same way back when he was around that age and first riding out to raid into Kansas.

When the racing was done, they all drifted back into the kitchen. The bluff game picked up where it had left off. Dunkle brought out a jug of corn doublings and passed it around.

With a full cup in his hand, Brade leaned back against the fireplace and rested his right foot on the roasting reflector. His thigh was still aching. It seemed to have gotten worse in the last few days. From all the riding, he supposed.

Sipping at the whiskey, he harked back to the attack the guerillas had made against the blockhouse at Fayette in 'sixty-four. They'd charged twice, and both times they'd been repulsed with volleys of fire from behind the loopholes. It had been a fiasco for the bushwackers. That was when he'd caught the ball in his leg.

It hadn't seemed like much of a wound then. Todd had cut the slug out for him. He'd bound it up with an old rag to stop the bleeding and then ignored it as best he could. He'd gone on riding, trying hard not to be bothered by the touch of fever he'd begun to feel.

The memories of several days of that expedition were muddled and broken. But the recollection of the stench of a festering wound was strong. So was the memory of flesh smoking and sizzling as the gangrene was burnt away with aquafortis. The surgeon had called it nitric acid.

He could almost hear that surgeon's soft voice with the odd twang. And his own agonized screaming. He'd felt shamed by that after it was all done. Worse shamed because the surgeon had been a Bluecoat in a damned Federal hospital. He still felt something of shame as he remembered.

The surgeon hadn't expected the aquafortis treatment to be successful, but he'd wanted to experiment, and it hadn't seemed to matter much when the patient was due to be hanged as a bushwacker anyway. But the acid had worked. Too well, as far as the Federals were concerned.

The surgeon considered his patient too lame to stand up. The guard knew that, so he didn't worry about dozing on watch. But the prisoner had been damned determined. He'd managed to walk out and steal a horse. That ride had been a hell-born nightmare, but it had gotten him to the home of Secesh sympathizers who were glad to hide and tend an injured Reb guerilla.

He'd still been hiding there, still too lame to go back to the fighting, when the war ended and the Federals finally ran down the Black Flag. He'd been one of the last to go in and accept the harsh terms of amnesty they'd offered to the guerillas. And that had been as painful to his pride as ever the wound was to his body.

Old scars ached as if the wounds had never really healed.

Despite the declarations of peace, the war in Missouri hadn't really ended. Likely the scar would always ache. Brade wondered if the war would ever be over. He wished to hell Logan would show up and explain what he was raising an army to do.

A while after noon the next day, Logan arrived. As soon as he'd turned in his horse and caught his breath, he called the men together.

Bob Alan Logan was the small-built, wiry kind of man who seemed always to be burning inside. A restless, tight-strung man who could stalk through the brush with the silent patience of a wildcat but who could never match his stride to the slow gait of a plow mule. His eyes were like pitch, hot and shiny in the kettle, about to boil, as he studied the men he'd called together.

"You've all been picked special," he began. "You're all men who fought in the war because you were good Confederates. You were hitting back at the jayhawkers and Yankees who invaded Missouri and took it away from you. And you've all had troubles with the damn charcoal Yankees since the war.

"Some of you've had your stock confiscated and your places burnt. All of you've had your right to vote taken away from you by the radicals in Jefferson City—"

It was Collis who interrupted, "Hell, almost everybody in the state's been disenfranchised. Under that Ironclad Oath, a man has to just about prove he never even spoke a kindly good morning to a Secesh sympathizer, or they won't let him vote or hold office or nothing."

"How'd you like to get rid of the Ironclad Oath? Maybe even the whole new state constitution the charcoals have put onto us?" Logan said.

"How do we go about doing that?" Collis asked back.

Brade muttered, "We can't exactly shoot down a constitution. Can't shoot every charcoal in Jeff City either."

"We can get 'em out of there though," Logan grinned. "All it takes is money."

Glancing around the room, Brade said sarcastically, "I reckon we might could raise ten or fifteen dollars hard money among the lot of us."

Logan's gaze fastened on him. "There's ways of getting money. You recall some news that happened up in Liberty in Clay County last February?"

That startled him. He stared back and asked, "You mean the bank robbing?"

Logan nodded.

"*You* didn't do that, did you?"

"No." He looked like he wished he had. "If the talk's true, that was a bunch from right up around there. Fellers who rode with us in the war."

Brade had a notion he knew which men Logan meant. There'd been a couple of brothers from up that way with Anderson at Centralia who'd been bold enough to try raiding a town on their own. He couldn't recall their names, but he remembered the young one's nervous blue eyes and quick hand with a revolver.

"Good Reb soldiers," Logan was saying. "They haven't given up the war just because Lee and Johnston quit back east."

"What the devil you getting at?" Brade asked him. "Are you saying we should join up with these Clay County boys and go back into guerilla fighting? You think the bunch of us could take over the state of Missouri and hold it against the rest of the United States?"

"Hell no! Not like that. What I'm saying is that we could go into the same kind of business to raise the money we'll need."

"What are we gonna need this money for?" Collis put in.

"First off, did you know that Adam McCoy is intending to run for governor next year?"

Logan held up his hands for silence, but it took a moment for the growling response to his question to die down. When he had their attention again, he went on, "We all know McCoy is the man behind Drake. McCoy's the one who did the most to put through the new constitution and the Iron-clad Oath, with all the damned things he's written up in that newspaper he owns. He's blasted hell out of ex-Rebs, and he's still making noises about how everybody who rode with the Irregulars should be outlawed again and shot down on sight. You know what it'll mean to us if he gets to be governor of this state."

The men clamored in response again. Somebody suggested shooting down Adam McCoy.

Logan answered, "Then his followers would claim that just proved how right he'd been. No, you got to fight politicians their own way."

"How?" Collis said. "Ain't a one of us got the knack for politics, far as I know. And none of us got a place to spread our ideas like McCoy has that newspaper."

"But I got a friend in St. Louis who has his thumbs in some pies in Jefferson City," Logan answered. "Greenback sorghum would do a lot to sweeten those pies. My friend is a man with political connections, and he knows how to *buy* votes. He knows other ways to put pressures on and get what he wants out of the state government, too. If we go along with this plan, raid maybe four or five banks this year and the same the next, come election time, *he'll* be the man who says which way for the wind to blow in Missouri."

"You mean he can get the charcoal radicals out of control?" Goforth said.

"I'll tell you this. He could keep McCoy from being elected governor."

"If we turn over the loot we plunder to him?" Brade added.

Logan looked at him darkly. "We share halves, that's all. He ain't asking more'n that. The money ain't all of it. He's got other ways to put the pressure on, once we start with the bank raiding."

"How?"

"It ain't something I can explain to you. You got to take my word for it."

Brade wished to hell he knew more about politics and such business. Logan made a twisty kind of sense. But for his own part, he'd rather fight a war where he faced his enemy over a gun. He asked, "Just who is this friend of yours?"

"I can't tell that. If any word of this deal was to get around, it'd ruin the whole thing. If his name was to get tied into it, he'd be ruined and so would we. You understand that, don't you?"

"I suppose so."

"What about it men? You want to fight for Missouri again?" Logan shouted, like an evangelist saving souls. He got a wild yapping of agreement. When it finally died down, he went on to say it would be soldiering, same as they'd done with Quantrill and Todd and Anderson. They were a company and needed officers.

They were unanimous in electing him captain, and there were no objections when he asked for Dunkle as a lieutenant.

"If you're all agreeable," he said then, "I'd like Bradenton for the second lieutenant."

Brade frowned in surprise. He'd never known Logan well. Why should the man pick *him?* He asked.

"You got a reputation for being steady and cold," Logan told him. "You're the one I'd like to have heading up the work inside of the banks while Dunkle and me lead things outside. You got a good name as a lieutenant under Todd. If you can handle things as good for us as you done for him, you're the officer I want. I expect the rest of the fellers will agree with me."

They agreed. And with that settled, Logan went on to outline his plan for their first attack.

CHAPTER 4

It was a cool and quiet Monday morning. At eight o'clock, the town of Serena had just begun to stir itself. The Rennert Savings and Loan Association opened its doors for another business day. A few people ambled along the walks on their way to work or to tend affairs. One lone wagon rattled past the bank, wheels screeing and trace chains jangling loud against the morning stillness. Nash came out of his store to sweep the walk. The straw broom made little swishing sounds on the planks, raising puffs of dust.

Behind the counter in the bank, Thomason Ready glanced up, frowning, as he swung open the vault door. That soft faraway rumbling he heard reminded him of cavalry troops, of horsemen on the move. It brought back vivid memories of his days with the Missouri Unionist Militia, chasing bands of wild marauders who'd plagued the state during the war years. He smiled at the reminiscence, although he was glad those times were past and the Rebs thoroughly put down. They should have hanged all those sons, he thought. Should have purged the state of every damned Secesh in it.

He snapped open his watch. Two minutes after eight. The assistant cashier was late to work again. He'd have to tell him off good—either change his ways or find work elsewhere.

The rumbling was growing louder and more distinct. He decided that it was a bunch of horses. Maybe drovers bringing a herd in for sale. Somehow it sounded ominous. They seemed to be galloping right onto the main street.

He opened the gate at the end of the counter and went through, meaning to take a look at whatever was going on out there.

The big front doors slammed open. Four men exploded into the bank with a yelping that sent icy chills of memory down his backbone. He stared at them—at ghosts from the war—four men in tattered blue cavalry blouses. Slouch hats pulled low shadowed their eyes. Kerchiefs masked their faces. And revolvers weighted their hands.

Ready's lips formed a word, but gave it no sound. It came out as a thin hiss. "Bushwackers!"

The man who strode toward him limped slightly. There was a Colt revolver in his right hand and an empty feed sack in the left. The bright calico scarf over his face muffled his voice, giving it a nightmare quality.

"Reckon we've come to make a withdrawal."

Ready couldn't find any answer. He stared at the pistol. It seemed to be staring back at him through that hollow black bore.

The masked man held the sack toward him, giving it a shake. "Suppose you fill this up. If it ain't big enough, we've got more."

There was no thought of obeying or disobeying. No thought of any kind. Ready stood in a stunned numbness and saw his own hand reach out to take the sack. It clutched the cloth in pale, trembling fingers. He felt his feet move, taking him behind the counter to the open vault.

Two of the bandits followed close behind him. The other two flanked the door. Ready saw them as if through a thin haze. The sounds of horses wheeling in circles and the yelping of the wild riders outside seemed far distant.

He swept the cash from the vault's shelves into the sack and held it out. The robber who limped took it. The other one said. "Don't I know you from somewhere?"

Ready shook his head.

"Sure. You rode with the Yankee militia, didn't you?"

"No!" he heard himself say.

The robber chuckled.

"Come on, let's get out of here," the lame one said, gesturing with his pistol.

The other one hesitated. Ready could feel the shadowed gaze and the threat it held. This man wanted to kill him—to shoot him down in cold blood—because of his soldiering during the war. His thoughts screamed. His mouth gasped a despairing, "No!"

"Come on!" the first bandit repeated in command. The other one moved then, backing through the gate as he kept his gun leveled on the banker.

Clear of the counter, both robbers wheeled and hurried through the door. Then the guards followed. From the street, Ready heard the shouts and the hard-pounding hooves. The horses stopped circling. They strung out, moving away fast. A sudden flurry of gunshots drowned all other sound for a moment. Then there was only a babbling of voices. Faces appeared at the open door of the bank. Questions reached toward him.

He turned his back to them. For the first time, he remembered the loaded horse pistol he'd stowed behind the counter after he'd heard about that robbery at Liberty. He looked at the open vault and the empty shelves. They became a watery blur. He clenched his eyes shut against the stinging of humiliation.

Beyond sight of the town, the riders separated. Singly and by twos, they spread out in different directions, Brade and Collis headed toward Marionville.

In the thick woods growing along a small creek, they drew rein, looked at each other, and laughed.

"That sure went smooth as cream," Collis said.

Brade nodded as he shrugged off the Army blouse. He pulled his suit coat from a saddle pocket and shook out the wrinkles.

"Just the way it was planned," he agreed. The raid had been sudden enough to shock and befuddle the townsfolk. The banker had been meek as a lamb. Not a shot had been necessary. The little powder that they'd burned had just been to spook a clump of people blocking the road out. And the feed sack was heavy with loot. Opening it, he began stuffing it into the saddle pockets.

"You see the look on that charcoal banker's face?" Collis asked, grinning.

"You really recollect him from the militia?"

He nodded, "I got a good eye for faces, and I seen a lot of them Home Guard right close up. He was one of 'em all right."

"Well, he's one that won't be sleeping easy tonight. A couple more raids like this and we'll have every money-grubbing charcoal banker in the state tossing awake nights worrying will he be next."

"Yeah." Collis relished the thought. "There was a few nights I laid awake myself listening for the sound of them jayhawk vigilantes coming to lynch me, like they done to some of the other boys. It's a real fine feeling to know there'll be charcoals worrying themselves the same way."

Mumbling agreement, Brade scooped the last of the loose coin out of the sack. He dropped most of it into the saddle pockets, then divvied the rest between himself and Collis. "You keep track of this. Want to keep it square with the rest of the fellers."

"What are you taking it out for?"

"Expenses. We got some time to kill before we head back to Dunkle's. Might be there's a decent tavern in Marlow where we can do some celebrating."

"Shouldn't we stay to cover?" Collis asked uncertainly.

"Us?" Brade mocked innocence. "What's a couple of good, honest farm boys like us got to stay hid for?"

"All right. You're the lieutenant," Collis said, pulling on his own suit coat. As he stepped up to his saddle, he added, "I just hope you're as smart as you think you are."

"What the hell you care? War's a getting-killed business to begin with."

"I'd sooner live through it."

Laughing, Brade put spurs to the bay's flanks. He leaned low over the horse's neck as he drove it into a hard gallop.

They eased pace before they reached Marlow and rode in quietly. It wasn't much of a town, just a crossroads with a few buildings clumped around. The tavern was the biggest of them.

There were men loafing in the taproom, some drinking, some just idling. None of them paid much attention to the newcomers. Evidently, the roads through town were well traveled enough that folk were accustomed to strangers.

Brade sipped at his beer, feeling the cold, restrained calm that wasn't really calmness at all but a tight-reined balance of tensions. He grinned at Collis in a lazy, relaxed way and lifted the mug in salute.

Behind him, the door slammed as someone suddenly rushed in. He turned to see what was happening.

A solid-built man with graying moustaches and a pistol in his belt skidded to a halt. Waving a yellow piece of paper, he hollered, "Boys, the bank at Serena's just been robbed!"

The loafers came alive. They crowded excitedly around him to hear the news.

"Just came by telegraph," he told them. "Law in Serena wants help. Says they were raiders like Quantrill's bunch . . ."

That brought a murmuring from the listeners.

"All dressed in stole Union uniforms, well armed and well mounted. If they're guerillas, likely they'll split up and head off every whichways. Might be some of 'em are coming this way. We got to get up a posse and meet 'em!"

"Yeah!" one of the loafers agreed with a grin. "We'll meet 'em all right. Decorate a few trees with 'em!"

Another asked, "Is there any reward offered?"

"It don't say. Might be, though."

"Reward or not, I'm gonna catch me a few," the hanging-minded man said.

"Well, don't just stand around talking about it. Fetch arms and horses, and let's get going!"

They broke, scurrying off, eager for the hunt. As the man with the telegram started for the door, Brade called to him.

"Hey, Mister, you reckon you could use a couple of extra men in this posse?"

He turned and eyed Brade critically. "We can use all the good men we can get. You're strangers around here, ain't you?"

"Just passing through. But we're traveling easy. No hurry to get where we're going. I reckon we can spare a while to ride along with you."

"You got weapons and horses?"

Brade nodded, shoving back his coat to show the butt of one of the Navy Colts in his belt. "Our mounts ain't as fresh as they could be, but the loads in our pistols are."

"You look well-armed."

"We do a mite of dealing in horses. Sometimes we're carrying a fair piece of cash money with us. Wouldn't want anybody trying to take it away from us." Brade grinned at him and hooked a thumb toward Collis. "My friend here is Abel Collis, and I'm Caudell Bradenton. We both of us got right strong feelings about bushwackers."

"Deak Helfer, deputy sheriff in these parts." He held out a hand. "Right pleased to have you join us."

Brade accepted the handshake. "My pleasure, Mister Helfer."

As the deputy hurried off to fetch his own horse, Collis tugged at Brade's sleeve and whispered, "What the devil you think you're doing! We ought to be getting away from here as fast as we can."

Brade shook his head. "They don't figure it's time enough for any of the robbers to have got this far. We're just nice friendly fellers eager to help hunt them no-good bushwackers. I'd sooner Helfer and his posse remember us that way than as a couple of well-armed strangers who disappeared as sudden as they showed up."

Collis failed to return his grin.

By the time the posse was ready to move out, there were some twenty men in it. Helfer split them up into threes and fours, telling them to spread out along the lanes and through the fields toward Serena. He called to Brade and Collis, "If you two don't know the land around here, you'd better come along with me."

They cut overland, picking up a creek and following it. Most of the bank was wooded. It was the kind of thick brush bushwackers took to. Brade studied the lay of the land, picking out likely places for a man to go to ground, trying to steer Helfer away from them. He didn't think anyone was hidden along there, but he couldn't see taking a chance on flushing a friend, if it could be helped.

He wasn't worried about the tumbled-down shanty standing by the water's edge. A man would be a fool to hide there, he thought.

But suddenly a lone figure broke from the shack, dashing toward the woods.

Helfer jerked up the shotgun he had across his saddle bow. And Brade slammed spurs to the bay's sides. He'd recognized Ron Goforth.

Lunging the horse, he raced past Goforth and swerved. He cut off the runaway's retreat—and put himself in Helfer's line of fire.

His hand on the rein was trembling as he pulled the bay to a halt. His body anticipated the impact of lead. He hoped to hell the deputy's reactions were quick.

The shout of warning eased the tension. He glanced toward Helfer, then looked down at Goforth.

As the bay blocked him, Goforth tried to wheel to the side. But Brade gigged the horse, blocking him again. He looked up then, and his jaw dropped. His eyes were fear and complete confusion as he stared at the revolver pointed toward his face. His startled grunt was an unshaped curse.

"Keep your damn-fool mouth shut, no matter what," Brade ordered in a harsh whisper. Louder, he snapped, "Lift them hands!"

Slowly, Goforth obeyed.

"Mister Bradenton, you could of got yourself killed!" Helfer called as he loped up. He looked pale around the edges, and Brade knew it had been close. "I had a bead on him—was squeezing the trigger—when you come right in line with my sights."

"Hell!" Brade made himself sound shocked, as if the idea had never occurred to him. But the sweat on his face and the slight shaking of his hand as he wiped at it were real.

Helfer took a deep breath, then turned to Goforth. "You're a bank-robbing bushwacker, but we got you now! And we'll get the rest of 'em too. We'll—"

"Dammit!" Brade grunted suddenly. Leaning out of the saddle, he peered close at Goforth's face, then called to Collis. "Come 'ere, take a look at this feller."

Collis heeled up his horse and gazed at Goforth uncertainly.

"That last town we stopped in 'fore we got to Marlow," Brade said, "Didn't we see this same feller there?"

"Huh?"

"You got a good eye for faces, Coll. Don't you recall seeing him in that last town?"

Collis caught on. He made a thoughtful humming in his

throat as he continued to stare at Goforth, then said, "Yeah, I recollect him. He was there all right."

Brade turned to Helfer. "I'm afraid this man couldn't no more be one of those bank robbers than I could."

The deputy grunted in disappointment. Shrugging, he spoke to Goforth. "Mister, next time a posse comes up on you, don't run 'less you've got reason to."

Goforth had finally collected his own wits. He mumbled, "How's I to know you're a posse? How'm I to know you waasn't a damn lot of thieves looking to rob *me?*"

"He's right there," Brade said. "We ought to have hollered a warning or something."

"Hell, it ain't easy to think straight when you're in the middle of man-hunting," Helfer muttered, gigging his horse. "Come on, we're wasting time here."

The other followed him, leaving Goforth standing and staring at their backs. After a few minutes, Brade had his hands steady again. He was completely calm, in that tight-strung way, when they spotted riders coming toward them. Helfer gestured for them to halt.

"You think that's the bushwackers?" Brade asked. Even at the distance, he knew that none of the riders were Logan's men. Part of a posse out of another town, he figured. They'd stopped, too, a ways beyond rifle range. He gazed at them, thinking that if they were from Serena, some of them might have been witnesses to the raid.

Warily, they began to move closer. Brade reminded himself that he and Collis had both been masked and wearing the Army jackets. The folks who'd glimpsed them on the streets of Serena wouldn't be likely to spot them now in their regular clothes with their faces bare. Even so, apprehension tingled through his fingertips as he watched them draw nearer.

Helfer sighed suddenly, a long gust of relief. "That's Sheriff Dooley in the beaver hat. They're from Serena."

Brade let himself grin. As Helfer started moving, he touched heels to the bay, keeping close behind the deputy. The two groups drew rein together, Helfer and Dooley greeting each other sociably. The sheriff eyed Brade and Collis curiously as Helfer introduced them, then began to introduce his own men.

Brade was watching their expressions, not paying much attention to the names, until Dooley said, "And Mister Orin Coleman from out to St. Louis."

Something inside Brade flinched. He gazed at the man Dooley indicated.

Coleman looked to be around thirty, a medium-built man in a plain black broadcloth suit. An ordinary-looking man. His moustache was a common cut and sandy-brown, a little lighter than his hair. His eyes were dull blue without much expression in them. He looked a little haggard and not much interested in man-hunting. In fact, he didn't look very interested in anything at all. That was what bothered Brade.

It seemed to him that if the man was as completely ordinary and innocuous as he appeared, he ought to be more excited about the robbery. Riding in a posse should have his nerves strung out. He should be showing signs of it, shouldn't he?

Brade had scanned him sharply, reading as much as he could as quickly as he could. He fastened his eyes on the two lawmen as they talked together, feigning an interest in what they were saying. He held the pose for a while, although he had a strong feeling of being watched and appraised.

Suddenly, he glanced toward Coleman. He saw the dull blue eyes blink. They gazed into the distance with no particular focus. But Brade was sure they'd been on him an instant before. He was certain that Coleman's interest in him was more than casual.

Helfer finished his talk with the sheriff. Turning to Brade and Collis, he said, "Looks like none of 'em came this way. Reckon we might as well give it up."

As soon as they were out of sight of the Serena posse, Brade took his leave of the deputy. He and Collis turned downroad at a fork, keeping a fair pace until they came to a water ford.

The horses nosed down, eager to drink. Brade stepped out of the saddle and bent to scoop up a handful of water for himself. He swallowed, then said, "Coll, I'm heading back toward Serena. You want to take the plunder and go on to Dunkle's?"

"You're *what?*"

"I got to follow that Orin Coleman. Got to catch up to him and ask him a few questions."

"In Serena?" Collis said incredulously.

"Yeah. I reckon that's where he'll be heading. He—" Brade stopped talking. He looked back over his shoulder, startled at the click of a gun scear.

Collis leveled a revolver at him. "You're *not* going to Serena. Not right now."

"You figure you can stop me with that?"

"This close up, I can stop you without hurting you too bad. I'd sooner see you shot up a mite than hanged altogether."

"Hell, Coll, I *got* to catch up with Coleman. You ain't stopping me by waving a pistol at me," he said, rising to his feet.

Collis studied on him, then stuck the gun back into his

belt. He sighed, "No, I s'pose not. But, dammit, Brade, this fight against McCoy is more important than any argument you've got with Coleman. We need you alive. We *can't* let McCoy get to be governor. We can't!"

Hesitating, Brade weighed his thoughts. He knew Collis was right. The fight for Missouri was more important than his own personal vengence. It was a hard decision.

He looked longingly into the distance toward Serena. It might be he'd never see Coleman again, he thought. Never run onto the man's tracks again. Never pay that debt. But he lacked for proof that Coleman was the man he wanted. And he *knew* Adam McCoy for his enemy.

"All right," he said reluctantly as he stepped up onto the bay. "Back to Dunkle's. On with the war."

CHAPTER 5

Several of the ex-guerillas being held in the jail in Richmond were old friends of Logan's. He intended to free them and add them to the gang. He swore he wouldn't leave Richmond without them.

It was easy enough to understand his feelings, but Brade didn't much like the idea of the jail delivery. The longer the raiders hung around a town when they hit it, the more danger there was. Townsfolk might come out of their first shock and start thinking about fighting back. This business was supposed to be a war against Adam McCoy and the charcoal radicals, not the people of Missouri. The raids were actions in that political war. Brade didn't want to see them turn into gun battles.

But Logan was determined to deliver his friends, so the plan was laid for Brade and Collis and four others to handle the bank while the rest of the men attacked the jail.

There were fourteen of them. They rode into Ray County quietly by twos and threes that May morning. They met together in the woods, changed their coats for the Army jackets, checked out their weapons, and headed into the town of Richmond a little before noon.

At the head of his troop, Logan laid spurs to his mount, shouting, "Charge!"

The yelping shouts and the wild shooting were as important as any other part of it. The riders plunged into town like so many demons just raised up from hell. They were a bomb exploding suddenly in the middle of the street. The shoppers and businessmen, the farmers and loafers who'd been drifting through an ordinary spring day scattered in panic as they struck.

Brade flung a shot toward a plate glass window. It shattered with a crash, showering clattering fragments of itself onto the walk. A blankly white face appeared for an instant where it had been, then disappeared even more quickly.

Jerking the bay to a rearing halt in front of the Hughes and Mason Bank, Brade waved for the others. Collis hurried up beside him as he strode across the walk. The Spring brothers, Dolph Ril, and Charlie Bees followed close at their heels.

The bank door was locked. Muttering a curse, Brade threw his shoulder against it. There was no yielding. Stepping back, he pointed the revolver at the lock and fired.

His thigh ached too much for him to do it himself. He hollered to Collis, "Kick that damn thing in, will you?"

Collis rammed a boot against the panels. The broken lock gave. The door slammed open. Catching his balance, Collis followed Brade's lunge through the doorway.

Brade scanned the stark, terrified faces of the tellers. Gesturing with the pistol, he said to Collis, "Take up the collection?"

Nodding, Collis shook open the feed sack and made for the vault. Brade stepped back, drawing the second revolver in his left hand. From the street, he could hear the horses milling, the men yelling, and random shooting. Then—suddenly—a volley.

What the hell was that? Something gone wrong with the jail delivery?

He took another backstep to Jake Spring's side. That was a fierce-looking weapon Jake held. A double-barreled revolver of some kind. He glanced at it, thinking he'd have to get a good look, when things were calmer. Huskily, he said, "You hold 'em a minute?"

Jake nodded, brandishing the gun at the pale-faced tellers, and Brade turned toward the door.

Lead slammed into the frame as he looked out. He felt the pinprick of a flying splinter against his cheek. Wincing, he jerked back.

He looked out more cautiously this time. The men in the street all were still mounted, keeping their horses moving as they fired. It wasn't random shooting. Their fire was being returned. White smoke rose in sharp puffs from behind hedges and trees. It wisped into the breeze from open windows.

The hell, Brade thought. He peered at one of the smoke-hazed windows. Sunlight cast the long thin shadow of a gun barrel across the whitewashed sill.

Lifting the right-hand revolver, he sighted along the hammer notch and lined up the muzzle pin with the window. But he knew it was no use firing. Half measures of powder just wouldn't kick pistol balls that far.

Easing back, he looked at the riders again. Dammit, some of them had carbines slung across their backs. Why weren't they on the ground behind cover using their sights against the enemy?

What enemy? This wasn't Lawrence, Kansas. It was Richmond, Missouri. And those were Missouri folk behind those guns. This war wasn't against them—it was *for* them.

But how the hell were they supposed to know that?

Collis gave a shout as he hurried toward the door with the full feed sack. Moving aside, Brade let him past, then dashed after him. Collis tossed the sack across the pommel and swung up onto his mare. Brade was on the bay, wheeling it, as the others from inside the bank mounted up. They clumped together, uncertain about the milling riders, wondering about the jail delivery.

Someone ran into the street. Brade glimpsed him, a middle-aged man in shirtsleeves, stopping suddenly there in the open.

Taking a stance, the man lifted a revolver. With a strange, time-locked clarity, Brade looked back along the barrel into the man's face. A plain, husky face with full moustaches and a clean-shaven jaw.

The revolver held as steady as if the man were setting his sights on a knothole. But Brade knew it aimed toward him. And suddenly he felt frozen—incapable of moving.

He seemed to hear the scear release and see the hammer begin its long fall toward the capped nipple. He flinched, expecting the impact of lead. But no fire and smoke spewed from the pistol. Instead, the man suddenly leaped up and back.

There was no change in the face, not even a wince of surprise, as he was flung back by the volley of shots that slammed into him. His shirt erupted splotches of bright red. He staggered. But he was still on his feet. He jerked up the other hand, locking it over the one that held the revolver. He struggled to keep it aimed. He fought the tension of the trigger spring.

Still caught motionless in the moment of awe, Brade stared at him. *The damned fool,* he thought. *God protect us from the damned fools!*

The weapon was dragging the man's hands down. It bucked, jerking itself out of his grip. The ball gouged dirt.

Slowly, the man bent forward. He looked as if he meant to reach for the dropped gun and try again. But the outstretched hand made no attempt to pick it up. The man fell. He lay face down in the dust and his own blood.

The trance broke. Wheeling his horse into the milling crowd, Brade shouted, "Let's get the hell out of here!"

"The jail!" That was Logan's voice. "We got to bust open the jail!"

Hell, hadn't they done that yet? The thoughts screamed themslves through Brade's mind. This whole thing was going bad wrong!

Logan waved, hollering as he drove his spurs into his mount's sides. He lunged it toward the jailhouse, with the others following. Brade swung the bay alongside.

Logan jumped down, shouting for the men to come with him. Brade stopped Collis and the Springs from dismounting. The ones who were afoot would need protection. They'd need the confusion of milling, firing horsemen between them and the townspeople.

He kept the bay moving, twisting in broken patterns and erratic turns. He flung lead in threat toward the hidden townsmen who kept up their fire at the raiders.

When the first revolver was empty, he switched it for the other. Six shots used, six more in hand. And the spare cylinder already loaded in his pocket. But it would take a few moments to disassemble a pistol and change the cylinder. He didn't want to have to do it on horseback under fire. He waved the second revolver but held stingy of using it.

Logan and his men were banging at the jail door, trying to break it open. They didn't seem to be having much luck. Swinging his horse back and forth in front of the jailhouse, Brade twisted between other riders. He feigned a charge directly toward a hedge hazed in powder smoke, reversing suddenly with a wild yelp.

A rifle spat in reply, the slug whining close past his face as he wheeled the bay. He charged again.

This time the sharpshooter broke from cover, dropping his single-shot rifle and running in jackrabbit leaps toward a building.

Brade jumped the bay over the hedge and saw the sniper disappear behind a quickly opened and slammed door.

As he turned back again, he glimpsed a man half-hidden behind the trunk of an elm, firing steadily and calmly. Not one man, he realized, just as a couple of raiders swung their horses toward the elm. Two—no—a man and a boy.

The riders charged, screaming as they fired.

The boy fell first. The man fell across his body.

Father and son, Brade thought. Somewhere there'd be a wife, maybe more sons and daughters.

The breeze twisted at wisps of powder smoke, but it wasn't strong enough to blow them away. Revolvers and guns roared out stinking masses of the white smoke. It hung in a thickening haze that stung in his nose and stirred memories. Above the hammering of hooves, the yelping of the riders and their weapons, he heard a woman scream. It was like Lawrence had been. Too damned much like Lawrence. This shouldn't be happening in Missouri—especially not by *their* hands.

Something moved. He saw the rifle barrel thrust out from behind a fence. *Keep your goddamned sights off me!* The shot he threw toward it was wild. But the rifle wavered and jerked back. He hadn't hit, but he'd scared hell out of somebody.

It seemed like an eternity had passed since Logan led his force to hammer at the barred door of the jail. But it looked like they hadn't made any way against it at all. Jerking the bay up near Logan, Brade shouted, "Dammit, ain't you done here yet!"

Logan looked up, mumbling under his breath. Then he looked passed Brade. Drawing a deep breath, he called out, "To hell with it! Everybody mount up!"

The men scrambled to their saddles. Flinging himself onto his horse, Logan raked it with his spurs. He plunged it past Brade, heading back the way they'd come.

The others strung out behind him, a rabble army in stolen uniforms. They rode hard, still shouting and throwing shots. Windows shattered. Swinging signs jumped at the slap of lead. Dogs yowled in reply to the yelps. Somewhere behind cover a man let loose an impressive string of profanity. One of the riders laughed wildly. From within a house, Brade could hear the panicked sobbing shrieks of a young child.

The sounds swirled together, churned with the thudding of the horses' hooves. They were a roaring in his ears, a thunder pulsing with the striding of his own mount. He bent low over the pommel, driving the bay, feeling the animal excitement that was in his own body echoed in the horse's gallop. But it was a sullen, uneasy excitement.

This was no withdrawal. It was retreat. A bitter, frenzied retreat. The raid had gone wrong. Everything was going sour. The whole damned war was stinking rotten.

There was no laughter and no talk when he and Collis separated from the others. And no pleasure in the food and drink they took at a quiet inn that night. Neither of them felt like celebrating.

When they reached Dunkle's, Logan wasn't there. He'd gone off to confer with his friend in St. Louis. The men loafed around the farm without plan or purpose, killing time at the bluff game and in arguments.

Brade was sick of hanging around the place. He just couldn't think of anything else to do, until word came that Adam McCoy was going to be speech-making in Lexington. He was electioneering for Charles Drake's campaign for the United States Senate. Considering on that, Brade decided to ride into town and take a look at the enemy. Collis and the Spring brothers bid to go along with him.

When they arrived, Lexington was slicked up in red-white-and-blue bunting, and the saloons were jam-packed. People had come from all over Lafayette and the neighboring counties for the parade and speeches. There'd already been an outbreak of fistfights. Armed soldiers patrolled the streets, trying to keep what peace was left, and the jail was full.

Sitting their horses at the hitch rack, the raiders watched over the heads of the throng as the parade broke up and Adam McCoy mounted the speakers' platform.

He was a long, lean man, like Jim Lane. His clean-shaven face was as sharp as a hatchet, with a knotty nose and a wide thin mouth twisted into a smug smile. When he doffed his hat to the cheering crowd, he showed off a haystack of soot-gray hair. He basked in their admiration. Despite his tall, bony build, he didn't really look much like Abe Lincoln, but as he posed, he seemed to be trying hard.

"Hell of a fine target," Little Spring muttered in a deadly soft voice.

Brade turned toward him. "You try it, and I'll put a ball into you before you can cock your pistol."

"Huh?"

"Anybody goes killing off McCoy that way, it'll make another John Brown out of him. That's just what we need."

"What the hell you talking about?" the kid snarled.

"There are a lot of folk in this state right now who ain't particularly interested in lynching every ex-Reb, but if McCoy was up and murdered the way Lincoln was, they'd sure start thinking about it."

"Man's talking sense," Jake admitted.

Little eased back then. Grumbling to himself, he watched the speakers' platform.

Collis leaned toward Brade. Thoughtfully, he said, "If

that's all so, ain't it likely them same folk are gonna get riled against us by our bank robbing?"

Brade considered the idea. "Could be."

"Maybe we're doing as much harm to ourselves as good by this raiding?" Collis suggested.

"Hell, I don't know! I ain't got a head for politics," Brade snapped back. There was sense in what Collis had said. Too much sense. It bothered him bad. Worse yet when McCoy got to talking about the Richmond raid.

The politician raved like a circuit preacher. He spun words, his voice dropping low, hushing the crowd, then shouting and rousing them to avid cheers.

He talked about the treacherous, murdering Rebs who'd tried to cut the heart out of Missouri. He hollered about Quantrill like he meant the devil himself. And when he'd finished stirring up ugly memories of the war, he turned his attention to the recent bank robberies, the Richmond raid in particular.

He managed to make it sound like a worse slaughter than ever the Lawrence attack had been described as. From the way he told it, men, women, and small children had been massacred in their beds and the town razed.

He spoke at great length about the thieves and murderers in their midst, making it clear he considered any Secesh sympathizer to be included under that heading. After that, he praised up Charles Drake and the part Drake had played in giving Missouri its new constitution and the Ironclad Oath. According to him, it protected the good people of the state from having Missouri taken over completely by fiends and traitors.

"Would you have the very men responsible for the atrocities in Richmond in the State House?" he declaimed.

"Had my way, they'd be in their graves!" someone shouted from the audience. A roar of cheering answered him.

Collis whispered, "I think we'd better get out of this town before the talking's over."

"Why?" Jake asked.

"I'll be damned surprised if there ain't at least one lynching around here after all this talk. I'd sooner it wasn't us."

Brade didn't like it. There was a miserable feeling to slinking away like minks. But it was better than being hanged. He yielded to Collis's arguments, and as McCoy made his final summation, they rode out together.

They traveled in moody silence into the twilight, wondering what was happening behind them in Lexington. And what would happen in the next town they raided.

CHAPTER 6

It wouldn't take them far out of the way, Brade told himself when he decided to go past his own land. He wasn't thinking about the Potter family—at least not to his own knowledge—until he spotted lamplight in their kitchen window. It was a warm, bright glow in the twilight.

Calling the others to follow, he turned onto the lane and halloed the house.

It was Mrs. Potter who answered him. Coming onto the stoop, she squinted against the sunset and asked, "Who's that with you?"

"Friends, ma'am. Just passing by and seen your light."

"Brade!" Amy shouted as she pushed past her mother. Clutching her skirts, she ran toward him. Coming up beside the bay, she grabbed his arm and got a foot atop his boot in the stirrup. The way she'd done when she was still in pigtails, she swung herself up to settle on the horse's rump and slide her arms around Brade's waist.

"Hey!" he hollered, startled.

Her mother snapped out, "Amy Potter!"

One of the Spring brothers chuckled. That stirred embarrassed anger in Brade. Twisting to look the girl in the face, he demanded, "What do you think you're doing?"

"You've been away so long," she said breathlessly. "I was afraid you were never coming back—I'd never see you again!"

Her arms were snug around him. He could feel their warmth, even through his coat. He tried hard to keep from grinning at her. As much as she bothered him, he couldn't help but take pleasure in her hug.

"You looking for Sam?" Mrs. Potter asked.

He nodded.

"He's not here right now. Went into town for some sort of speechmaking. Likely he'll be back soon. You and your friends want to wait, maybe take some food?"

"We'd be obliged."

"I suppose you can bed in the barn, if you want," she added. She scowled at Amy, "You fetch down here, come help me set up something for these men to eat."

"But, Ma . . ."

"Amy, you heard your ma," Brade said sternly.

Sighing, she slid down off the horse and hurried into the house, with her mother close behind her.

"That's a right pert piece," Little muttered.

Brade snapped, "You keep your mouth shut about her."

"You got claim on her?" the boy asked.

"No."

"She kin of yours?"

"No."

"Then don't you tell me nothing what I can say about her. She's right pert. I'll bet she's lively, too!"

"I told you to shut up about her!" Brade hollered, wheeling the horse toward him.

"Like hell I—!"

"Let's get the horses tended," Collis interrupted. Jake agreed. Little yielded to his brother, falling silent. And Brade said nothing more as he led them to the barn.

The women were busy at the stove when they walked into the kitchen. Mrs. Potter gave them a quick smile in response to Brade's introduction. She remembered Collis from Todd's band and welcomed the others as if she'd known them, too. But despite her smile, Brade could sense the tension in her.

She looked at him as he walked over to pull a chair out from the table and settle himself. "Your leg bothering you again, Brade?"

"No, ma'am."

"You're walking lame."

"I am?"

She nodded. "Maybe it's the weight of the pistols you're carrying that's bothering you."

He didn't have an answer for that. Stretching out his legs, he crossed his ankles and gazed at his boot toes.

Collis took a place at the table. He sat there, looking around as if he hunted words to fill the sudden silence. He didn't find any.

It was Little Spring who spoke up. "That's beef stew, ain't it, ma'am? It sure does smell good."

She smiled at him. "You set yourself to the table. There'll be a heap of it for you soon as it's warm enough."

Grinning, he took a place. Jake settled beside him. He watched Amy moving around, putting out saucers and cups.

But she was looking at Brade. "Where you been all this time?" she asked him.

"Away."

"I know that. Where?"

"China," he grumbled.

She poked him in the ribs.

"Hey, don't do that!" he snapped at her. But he couldn't help grinning.

She turned sharply away, giving her skirts a twirl. Little watched her with an expression that faded Brade's grin. He was beginning to be sorry he'd brought that colt around here.

The sound of a wagon rattling up the lane sent Mrs. Potter scurrying out. As soon as she was gone, Little looked to Amy. "You got a real pert ma."

She nodded.

"You sure take after her."

Color flooded the girl's cheeks. She smiled at him for an instant before she turned away.

After a few moments, Potter came in with his wife. He settled across from Brade, eyeing him. "I've been into town listening to this Adam McCoy feller talk."

"We were there for most of it."

He looked surprised. "Didn't think you'd take kindly to McCoy."

"I don't."

"He's got folks right riled up."

Brade nodded.

"You ain't come around here to take up on your land again, have you?" Potter asked.

"Not right now."

"You planning to?"

"You sound like you don't much care for the idea."

Silence filled the room again. Collis cleared his throat, the sound too loud. He said nothing, but slumped deep into his chair as if he could hide in it.

Potter took a spoon out of the glass on the table. He twisted it in his fingers, gazing at it. "I'll tell you the truth, Brade. I don't. Mind you, I got nothing against you personal. I mean I like you, but I don't want no part of the trouble you got around you."

Jake Spring stiffened, his eyes narrowing on Potter.

Soft-voiced, Brade said, "I thought you were pulling out of here."

"I give it a lot of thought. I went over what you'd said about a man being run off his land. I don't *want* to leave here. Way I figure, the ones that burnt you out, it was *you* they're after. I think long as you ain't around here, they won't come bothering me. But if you build up your place again, and I'm friends with you, it might be your trouble would spill over onto me and mine. I don't want that."

"I ain't planning to stay around here," Brade answered. "If you want, I'll get out now."

"Pa!" Amy's voice was hurt and pleading.

Her father glanced at her, then looked to Brade again. "Don't take me wrong, boy. The missus says you want to eat and put up here tonight. I don't mind that none, as long as there ain't any posse after you . . ."

"What give you the notion there might be a posse after us?" Little growled.

Brade snapped, "You stay the hell out of this!"

"Dammit, you stop ordering me around. I'm getting sick and tired of you and your damned orders!" The boy started to his feet, his fists clenched.

Brade eyed him coldly.

Grabbing his arm, Jake said, "You better set down, little brother."

It was obvious that the kid didn't want to. But Jake was boss in the family. Little slumped into his chair, scowling.

Potter gazed at Brade, but he got no answers to his unspoken questions. Mrs. Potter ladled out helpings of the stew, and Amy carried them to the table. Her eyes were inquiring, too, as she looked at Brade. He refused to meet them.

It was an awkward meal, with spurts of feeble talk and long empty pauses. When it was finally over, he hustled the men outside. Jake headed for the outhouse, with Little trailing after him. Collis followed Brade into the barn, and they settled by the lantern to clean their guns. When Jake came in, he joined them, pulling the fierce double-barreled pistol out of its belt scabbard.

"What kind of thing is that?" Brade asked him.

"LeMat."

"French-made, ain't it?" Collis said.

Jake nodded sullenly. But his pride in it got the best of him. He began to show off the weapon. "Forty-two caliber nine-shot cylinder for this top barrel. And the bottom one loads buckshot. Hammer's hinged so's you can fire whichever you want. See? Jeb Stuart carried one like it."

He held it out for Brade to admire, then began to strip it down. He had it in pieces when Brade glanced around, then said, "Little ain't come back yet."

"He'll be along."

"He's a mite hair-sprung, ain't he?"

"He's all vinegar," Jake grunted. "Real good boy. You go pushing him, he'll kick."

"I ain't pushing him."

His eyes narrowed on Brade. "You sure don't give me the notion you *like* him."

"Do I have to *like* him?"

"You damn well better not start no trouble with him, else you'll have the both of us to answer to."

"He better not start no trouble," Brade matched his tone, "else you'll both have *me* to answer to."

"You reckon you're the devil with the hair still on?"

"I reckon—shush!" Brade cocked his head, listening intently. Collis frowned at him in question. The strange sound came again.

"What the hell is that?" Collis whispered.

Brade thought he knew. He held back a grin and said, "What's it sound like to you?"

It came again, a dull plink and brief whine. Collis concentrated. "Damn if it don't sound like a banjo tuning."

"Yeah." Brade let himself grin then. He heard five plinks, climbing in tone as fingers tested the strings. It was tuned up to snuff.

"That's Little," Jake told them. "Where the hell you s'pose he got a banjo?"

"Potter's got an old whittled one," Brade said, standing up. "What I want to know is what he's doing with it in the middle of the night."

He climbed down and paused outside the barn door. The moon spilled pale light, but the shadows were black as pitch. It took him a moment to see Little by the wash shed, setting up on the battling board, his legs dangling and the banjo in his lap. Tilting back his head, the kid began to sing.

The tune wasn't familiar. Brade caught a few words, something about hating Yankees. Amused, he moved closer silently.

"I can't take up my musket to fight 'em anymore, but I ain't gonna love 'em, that's for certain sure, and I don't want no pardon for what I done and am, and I won't be reconstructed, and I do not give a damn!"

Finishing his song, Little gave the banjo a hearty whomp and laughed. Someone else laughed with him.

It was Amy's voice, bright and happy, and it halted Brade as if a fist had rammed into him.

"Where on earth did you get that?" he heard her ask.

"Feller in Warsaw was singing it. Old soldier feller had himself a wood leg," the boy said. "Why don't you set here next to me and I'll sing you another'n."

Anger burned in Brade's throat as he strode toward them. "Amy! What the devil you think you're doing? Your folks got any idea you're out here in the middle of the night?"

"Caudell Prescott Bradenton!" she answered from the shadows. "You sure come butting in sudden, don't you?

"Your folks know you're out here?"

"I swear, you're just as bad as Little says you are, always

ordering people around." There was a teasing sullenness in her voice.

"Look here, *Lieutenant,"* Little slid off the battling board and set down the banjo. He faced Brade. "You keep your damn nose out what ain't your business!"

Ignoring him, Brade snapped at the girl again, "Amy, you answer me!"

"You know my folks can't stop me of anything I got my mind set on! *You* can't stop me either. *You* got no claims on me, Caudell Bradenton! You go away, leave me and Little be!"

Rising, she stepped to Little's side and pressed her shoulder to his. Their figures merged against the skyglow.

"You stay back. I'll settle this," Little muttered, making his voice loud enough for Brade to hear too. "I'll string him down a mite."

"You think you can string me down, come on and try."

The boy lifted his fists and started toward Brade.

"No! Don't!" Amy squealed.

Brade lunged a left under Little's guard. It caught him just below the breast bone. As his mouth dropped open, Brade's right came up under his jaw. Slowly folding at the waist, he collapsed.

Brade wheeled, grabbing Amy by the wrist. "I ought to turn you down and tan you good!"

"No! You got no right—you leave me alone!" She wrenched against his grip. But he held tight, jerking her toward him.

"What the devil you mean coming out here with him like this?" he demanded.

She snuffled, then said, "It wasn't anything. He was just going to sing me some songs. That's all."

"Sure, like hell. You listen to me—you stay away from him and the likes of him."

"He's *nice.* He's real nice, the way you used to be back before you got so mean!" She twisted against his grip again.

"All right, I'm mean. So is Little Spring. You stay the hell away from both of us." He dragged her toward the house.

"No!" she protested. "You're going away again, ain't you? Please, Brade, don't go away!"

He gave her no answer.

Snuffling again, she said, "Do you *have* to go away?"

"Yeah."

"Then take me with you!"

"The hell!"

"I won't be any trouble. I can cook for you and mend and

everything. I'll be good. I'll do whatever you tell me, Brade. Please take me with you!"

"You'll do whatever I tell you *now*. You'll get into that house and go to bed like you belong. You'll stay inside while we're around, and if you speak one more word to Little Spring, it'll be a week before you can sit down comfortable again. I'll promise you that!"

"No," she repeated, but this time there was no conviction in her voice. He pushed open the kitchen door and shoved her through it.

"I'll get even with you, Caudell Prescott Bradenton," she grumbled as he slammed the door shut.

He went back to Little. Heaving the unconscious boy over his shoulder like a sack of grain, he carried him into the barn and dumped him in the loose straw on the floor.

"What's that?" Collis called from the loft.

"Little fell asleep outside. I fetched him in."

"Fell asleep!" Jake echoed.

"Yeah, that's what I said," Brade grunted as he started up the ladder. "You doubting me?"

Jake eyed him suspiciously, but answered, "I'll wait till I hear it from Little. Only if he tells me different, you got trouble."

Settling to finish capping the revolvers, Brade said, "Trouble don't bother me none."

Jake snorted through his nose and started down the ladder. As soon as he was out of earshot, Collis whispered to Brade, "You mind out for them two. 'Fore you're through, you're gonna tangle with 'em."

He nodded in silent agreement. The way things were headed, it sure looked that way.

When he woke the next morning, Collis told him the Spring brothers were gone.

"Decided they don't want to ride back to Dunkle's with us. Said they're going to Independence and enjoy some of the money they've made. Said they'd be along to Dunkle's in a week or so."

"That's fine with me," Brade grunted.

Collis moved his mouth, cleared his throat and started, "Brade, this place—them folks—truth is, I'm getting homesick. I'd kinda like to go by, visit my family myself."

"Hell, why not? Go ahead, if you want."

"You won't get into trouble?"

Brade almost snapped at him. But he knew Collis meant well enough. Sighing, he answered, "You want me to swear to it? What kinda trouble am I gonna get into?"

"I dunno. I just got this feeling—"

"To hell with it. You want to go home, go ahead," he worked up a grin he hoped would be reassuring.

Collis grinned back, then hurried down from the loft to saddle his horse.

Following him down, Brade went on into the yard. The sun was already poking up over the trees. Its glare hit him in the face. Squinting against it, he went to the well and hauled down the sweep.

The water in the bucket was icy cold. As he slapped handsful of it into his face, he heard the kitchen door open. Wiping at his eyes with his knuckles, he blinked and saw Amy come into the yard.

She looked toward him and called tentatively, "Brade? You want some breakfast?"

"No!"

Pouting, she snapped back, "Well, it's too late now. Everybody else ate already."

He watched her slam the door behind her. She'd been trying to make up last night's argument, he thought, but he'd refused. Maybe he'd been wrong. Maybe he should square things away with her before he left. Leastways, he had a strong urge to try.

He went on into the kitchn. She was there at the stove when he walked in. Shooting him a quick glance, she repeated, "You're too late for breakfast."

"I ain't hungry," he said, with a sound of apology. "But I sure could stand some coffee."

She tried to hide her smile as she pushed the pot over the fire, but he caught a glimpse of it. He grinned a bit himself. Reaching for a cup, he said, "You sure got a knack for getting a man riled."

"You're turning *mean.*" She kept her back to him. "Just as mean and stubborn as Old Ned."

"It ain't proper for you to go walking out at night like that with a feller you don't even know," he said.

"I know him! He's just like you. Like you *used* to be."

This getting compared to Little Spring was beginning to rankle him. He answered harshly, "If that's so, when he's my age, he'll be mean and stubborn like me!"

She turned toward him then, looking sorrowful. "Brade, I didn't mean—I just—you—"

"You sure don't sound like you hold much with me these days," he muttered.

"I don't hold with you running off with pistols in your belt and not a word to anybody about where you're going or what you're doing. I don't know if you'll ever come back. For all I know, you're off hurt or dead in a gulley somewhere. How do you expect me to feel about you?" Her chin began to quiver.

"I don't expect it to make *you* no difference. What *I* do is none of your business. You go chase yourself some man who wants to settle down with a wife and kids."

"You want to! Don't lie to me, Caudell Prescott Bradenton, that's just what you want, and you know it!"

Damn her, but she could kick. He grumbled, "If that coffee gets much hotter, it'll boil over."

She wheeled away from him. Jerking up a potholder, she pulled the coffee off the stove. She was snuffling as she tilted the pot over his cup. She poured a cup for herself, too, and sat down across from him.

He sipped at the coffee. After a moment, he asked, "Amy, you got any idea what Little Spring was thinking when you walked out with him like that?"

She nodded, not meeting his eyes.

"What the hell were *you* thinking?"

"I got my reasons," she mumbled.

He wondered if she did. But she was only a little girl. She had no business walking out with Little. She had no business chasing after *him* the way she did either. If she *had* to hunt after a man, it should be a nice steady boy like she'd get to know at Sunday meeting, not some damned bushwacker.

She had to be broke of these fool notions once and for all, he thought. Maybe if he could hurt her deep—get her really mad at him—

"You had your reasons," he said darkly. "Maybe Little ain't the first one you've been walking out with? Maybe you know all about it? How much time *you* been spending in the bush?"

"Brade!"

"That why you wanted to come along with me? You're one hell of a little bitch, ain't you?"

She swung up out of the chair, her face reddening. Her eyes on his were moist, pained. "Brade, you don't—?"

"I know your kind," he said.

She wheeled away from him. With a sobbing gasp, she flung herself through the door and slammed it behind her.

Well, that was that, he told himself. He'd shook her of the damn-fool admiration she'd had for him. Maybe now she wouldn't be so quick to fancy the next feller who reminded her of him.

He swallowed the last of the coffee and stood up. Limping, he headed out to collect his horse. As he stepped to the saddle, he heard Potter call to him from the house. Ignoring him, he jabbed spurs to the bay and galloped toward the road.

CHAPTER 7

Things were quiet at Dunkle's. Several men were off visiting their families. A few of the others were in towns, spending their shares of the bank plunder. Logan was away on business. Only Dunkle, Ron Goforth, and Bill Archer were there when Brade arrived.

Almost two weeks had passed when the Spring brothers showed up. Brade was sitting on the bench by the horse pen cutting a new cheek piece for his bridle when he spotted them coming.

They had someone with them. A girl riding astride a man's saddle on a sorrel filly. Amy Potter. Drawing up in front of the house, Little swung off his horse and hurried to give Amy a hand down. She got her leg over the pommel and slid awkwardly out of the saddle into his arms. They both laughed.

There was a cutting edge to the laughter. It gashed into Brade's mind like a mill saw, shredding his thoughts and scattering them. It left only hot rage as he dashed toward them.

Little mocked a gallant bow. With a hand on Amy's arm, he led her toward the door. He was grinning, chattering at her. The chatter stopped abruptly. He turned, his face open in surprise and stark fright the instant before Brade struck.

Brade was aware of his fist ramming toward the kid's gut. He saw the face twist, melting into a blur. He heard Little's squeal of pain. And Amy's terrified scream.

The anger in him was numbing, blinding. He felt the wrongness of his blow without understanding it. He was only vaguely aware of the sudden streak of red across Little's shirt.

His arm was swinging back, his shoulder set to drive the fist at the kid again, when something slammed into him. It rocked him. He staggered back, off balance.

The wild bull bellow was Jake Spring's. It was Jake lunging against him, throwing him down. He fell with Jake sprawling across him.

He tried to heave his fist toward Jake's ribs.

Flinching ahead of the blow, Jake rolled away from it. Freed of his weight, Brade started to his feet. He could hear Amy's shouts for help and running footsteps, but they were distant and meaningless. There were no thoughts in him—only rage. He meant to go for Little again—to hammer his fists into the kid, to beat him down.

Through a haze, he saw the boy standing, bent forward, both hands pressed up against his chest. Behind the spread fingers, his shirt gaped open across the breastbone. The bare flesh under it was smeared with a bright red that stained the cloth and spilled onto his hands. His face was clenched into a knot of pain. A low moaning rolled in his throat.

The blood puzzled Brade, jerking him to a halt. He was overwhelmed with the sense of wrongness.

Amy was staring at him, her eyes wide with horror. Her lips moved, but there was no sound from them. They shaped an accusation of something he didn't understand.

Then he discovered the knife in his hand. The blade was smeared with blood. Shocked, he let it slide out of his fingers.

Jake Spring was suddenly in front of him. Jake's face was a thunderhead of anger, about to burst. The twin-barreled French revolver was in his hand, its muzzles leveled at Brade's face.

The dam that held Brade's thoughts frozen broke. In a wild rush, he knew the whole of it. He'd hit Little without being aware he had the knife in his hand. He'd cut the kid, maybe bad. And now Jake was holding vengeance a hand-span from his face. Nine lead slugs and a barrel of buckshot.

He could see the white knuckled tension in Jake's fingers. The pistol quivered in the hard-locked grip as his thumb jerked back the hammer. The forefinger began to close on the trigger.

In an instant that was drawn out to a fine-honed eternity, Brade gazed at the gun. In the same instant, his mouth was thick with the taste of wanting to stay alive. His mind screamed for him to find the way.

The marrow in his bones was ice. His muscles were dried cracked leather, as stiff as plate iron. It felt as if there'd never be any response to the order he flung at them.

The world exploded around him.

He was throwing himself downward as everything flew into sharp-edged shards of sound. They speared into his skull, crackling and rolling like ball lightning. A burning claw scraped at his scalp, trying to rip it off. His eyes clamped themslves shut, filling with reddish flares. He felt himself falling.

His arms wrapped onto something—Jake Spring's knees. He was hauling Jake down with him. He knew Jake hit the ground with a hard thud. He could feel it. But he couldn't hear it above the violence of the thunder still echoing inside his head.

Forcing against knotted muscles, he got his eyes open. The revolver was in Jake's grip. He swung at it. The side of his open hand rammed across Jake's wrist. The gun went flying from his fingers.

Brade rolled and rose to his feet. The world had gone wild. It was a blurred nightmare of pale faces seen through a reddish haze. The roaring in his head drowned any sound but itself, filling his skull with pain.

Jake was scrambling up, his mouth working violently. Brade couldn't hear whatever came out. But that didn't matter right now. Jake was plunging toward him. Wheeling to the side, he jerked up a hand. Jake was bent forward, head down, as he attacked. Brade twisted away, chopping down, open-handed. He caught Jake at the back of the neck. Jake took one more step, then collapsed on his face in the dirt.

Brade gazed at the blurred figure. Blinking, he tried to clear his vision. He stood with his legs spread against the rocking of the earth under him. There was still no sound except the roaring in his head. It was like water through a mill race, pounding on him, pouring itself over him, threatening to drown him.

Someone held out an arm. The big man, Bill Archer, he thought as he leaned against it. He tried to say something, but he couldn't hear his own voice. Weakly, he slid into darkness.

He woke lying on his quilts in the dark corner of the barn he'd claimed for his bed. He was alone in a musty, pain-filled dusk. His head hurt like hell. He could hear sounds from the horse pen and the yard, but they were muffled and faint, seeming off pitch. He felt as if he were trapped somewhere within a vague and ugly dream.

If he'd seen anyone around, he'd never have allowed himself the luxury of groaning. But he was alone, and there was some relief in making a sound and being able to hear it, even if it did have a wrongness to the tone. Whatever might be wrong with his head, at least he wasn't deaf.

That revolver of Jake's had gone off damned close.

Aching all over, he dragged himself up and staggered out into the yard. The sun was low, half-hidden behind the trees. He'd been unconscious for a good part of the day.

Squinting into the shaving mirror by the sluice, he found that his face was caked with dried blood. When he dabbed gently at it with a handful of icy water, most of it washed away. There seemed to be a couple of shallow gashes at the hairline on his left temple. And a patch of hair about the size of his palm was singed to stubble. The dark smear on his forehead didn't wash away. He realized it was gunpowder, flecks of it embedded in his skin. The buckshot had barely scraped him, but the muzzle flash of the LeMat had been too damned close.

He sloshed more water into his face. Studying his reflection in the mirror, he wondered if that gunpowder brand would eventually wear off.

There was blood on his shirt. There'd been blood on Little Spring's shirt, too. How bad had he cut the kid? He sure as hell hadn't meant to do that. Turning, he limped toward the house.

The whole downstairs was empty, but from above he could hear hammering. He found Bill Archer in the upstairs hallway with a mouthful of nails, doing something to one of the bedroom doors.

Mumbling through the nails, Bill said, "You up and around already? How you feel?"

Brade heard the words clearly enough, but strangely. His ears felt numb. Leaning his shoulder against the wall, he answered, "My head's cracked open. How's Little?"

"Not bad off. You sure whomped Jake one, though. He ain't come around yet. They're both bedded down." Archer nodded toward a closed door down the hallway. "That little girl's tending to them like they was her kinfolk."

"The hell!" Brade looked suspiciously at the hammer in Archer's hand. "What you doing there?"

"Putting a bar on this door for the little lady. This is the best room in this broken-down place."

"Don't bother. She ain't staying the night."

"She says she is. She says she intends to stay here and nurse Little till he's well. Seems to think somehow it was *her* fault you cut the boy." Archer eyed him as if to ask was that so and why.

He wasn't planning to answer that question. Turning from Archer, he headed down the hallway. The door opened before he reached it. Dunkle slipped out, closing it behind him. Glaring at Brade, he growled, "What the devil got into you?"

"He hadn't no business bringing her here. No damned business seeing her at all."

"Is she *your* business, Lieutenant?" Dunkle raised a curious eyebrow. "You got some claim on her?"

"I'm friends to her folks. And I'm taking her back to them tonight."

"You're going to have a wildcat on your hands if you try taking that gal anywhere against her will."

"I'm taking her back," Brade said stonily.

Dunkle shrugged. Slyly, he said, "Go ahead."

Brade shoved open the door. Amy was settled in a chair between it and the bed where both Jake and Little were stretched out. Ron Goforth sat in another chair on the other side of the bed. He looked up as Brade stepped in. Making a shushing sound, he gestured toward the bed. Both Springs were asleep.

Amy turned. She came up out of the chair at the sight of Brade. Her eyes were wide and uncertain, questioning him.

"Come on, you're going home," he said harshly, reaching for her arm.

She jerked back, suddenly defiant. "No!"

"Come on," he repeated.

She shook her head. "You stay away from me, Caudell Prescott Bradenton!"

"Amy—" Even in the twilight half-dark, he could see hot sparks in her eyes.

"Don't you touch me! Don't come near me! Not after what you did to Little!"

"Listen to me, Amy! You're—"

"Miss Amy don't want you bothering her," Goforth interrupted, rising. He stiffened his shoulders as he stepped around the foot of the bed. His hands clenched at his sides. "You heard her, she wants you to leave her alone."

She bobbed her head in agreement.

Brade heard the door behind him open. Dunkle came in, grinning slightly, and asked with mock innocence, "Trouble, Lieutenant?"

"She's going home," Brade said.

"No, I'm not! And *he* can't make me, can he?" she looked to Dunkle.

"If she wants to stay here, she's welcome," he answered. "That's what I say."

"Me too," Goforth put in.

"I mean to stay here and take care of Little," she said triumphantly.

Dunkle's grin broadened. "Looks like you're outvoted, Lieutenant. Maybe you'd better do like the lady wants and just leave her be."

Brade realized there wasn't much use in fighting. Not against both these men and Amy as well. He had a feeling that even if he dragged her out by the hair and herded her home at gunpoint, she'd never stay put. She'd ridden in, and she'd be able to find her way back now. If this was what she wanted, let her have her own damn-fool way, he told himself. He felt too damned weary to argue about it. His head hurt too much for thinking. Let her tangle with Little Spring, if it was what she wanted. If she didn't have sense enough to look out for herself, it was none of *his* business.

"Sure," he mumbled. "I'll leave her be. And *she* can damn well stay away from *me* while she's around here."

He stalked into the hall, slamming the door behind him.

Archer let up his hammering to ask, "Change your mind, Lieutenant?"

Brade held back an angry reply. Instead, he studied thoughtfully on the big man. "Archer, you got a girl about her age, ain't you?"

Archer nodded.

"How'd you feel if your child ran off to a bunch like us?"

"We ain't such a bad sort." He swept the nails out of his mouth and looked intently at Brade. "She strikes me as a right nice girl. Lot like my Beth. I reckon that's why I'm fixing up this room for her. I mean to look out for this little girl, just the same as if she was my Beth. I'll see to it every man around here knows that, Little Spring included. *You* included, too."

He really meant it, Brade thought. And this hulking bear of a man could back up his words. Likely Archer could do a damnsight better job of looking after Amy than he could, especially with the troubles that had come between him and the girl.

Nodding, he said, "You do that."

Archer grinned. "Long as we all understand each other."

As Brade headed downstairs, he heard the hammering begin again behind him. There was reassurance in the sound. He felt a deep relief at Archer's promise to protect the girl. The responsibility wasn't all on him now. But hell, why did she have to be so stubborn about going home? Why did she have to come here in the first place? Why did one trouble have to pile onto another until a man felt like the weight of them could crush his bones?

He stumbled out to the barn and dropped onto his quilts. It would all be a lot easier, he thought, if only the damned pain in his head would go away.

It was well after sunrise when he woke. And his head still hurt. Getting up didn't seem worth the bother. He lay half-dozing for a long while before the sound of footsteps at the barn door disturbed him into wakefulness again.

Propping himself on one elbow, he watched the door edge cautiously open. Amy Potter peered in.

"What the hell you want?" he growled at her.

"I—they said this is where you slept. You never came for breakfast." She was carrying a cup. Holding it out in both hands, like a peace offering, she said, "I thought you might want some coffee."

"You reckon you can fetch me that and I'll say thanks and forgive you coming out here with Little Spring?"

"I only thought—maybe—I—oh, you go to hell!" Flinging the coffee on the ground, cup and all, she wheeled to run away.

"Amy!" he called after her. He hadn't meant to. It just happened before he could stop himself.

She looked hopefully over her shoulder at him.

He didn't know what he wanted to say. He muttered, "You got no business hanging around this place."

"I've got to see to it that Little gets well now," she snuffled. "You shouldn't have took a knife to him that way, Brade!"

"What'd you expect me to do? Welcome you here with him?"

"I didn't expect you to try to kill him!"

"Didn't mean to. Only meant to whomp him good. You're the one I ought to whomp."

She stiffened her spine and cocked back her head, thrusting out her chin defiantly. "What *I* do is none of *your* business, Caudell Bradenton!"

He didn't want to grin. He couldn't help it, though. Damn her, but she had a way about her. He said, "You left out the Prescott."

"Huh?"

"Generally, you give me both barrels when you mean to nail up my hide."

"Generally, I *what?* Oh—" Suddenly she smiled. "What makes you think I want to nail up your hide, Caudell *Prescott* Bradenton?"

He told himself it was all wrong to go getting friendly with her again. It didn't seem like he could stop himself of it, though. "You're an ornery little girl. You *knew* you'd be stirring up trouble, coming out here with Little Spring."

"You called me mean names. You shouldn't have done that, Brade. You didn't mean it—you *know* you didn't! I had to come see you again."

"Coming here with him, you give me a notion you deserve the names I called you."

She shook her head. "You don't mean that either."

He sighed wearily, "Well, you've seen me again. Now you'd better let me take you on home."

"No. Not now—not after—" She paused and drew herself up again. "I'm going to stay here and look after Little while he's hurt. I'm going to cook for you all and do mending and things. I talked to Mister Archer about it. He's nice. He fixed up a room for me, and I'm going to stay here. They all agreed I could."

"All but me," he muttered, sitting up. He leaned his arms across his knees as he studied on her. "Amy, you got any idea what our business together is?"

"Springs told me all about it," she answered, almost breathless with enthusiasm. "You're fighting for Missouri again, like you did with George Todd!"

"Todd's dead."

"I'm not afraid. I want to fight for Missouri, too. Just because I'm a girl, nobody thinks I can *do* anything. But Dick Maddox' wife rode along some of the time in the war, didn't she?"

"You're damn well not riding with us!"

She snuffled slightly. "Well, maybe I can't *ride* with you, but I can help here. And I don't care what you say—I'm staying!"

"Look, Amy, your folks are going to be worried sick about you," he tried.

"I left them a note, told them I was coming to you. They know you'll look out for me," she said with absolute certainty.

"Oh hell!" If there was an argument that would win against her, he sure couldn't think of it now. He rubbed a hand at his face. His head ached something awful.

She waited a silent moment. Then, picking up the cup, she said, "You want some coffee, Brade?"

"Yeah," he grunted in weary defeat.

"I'll fetch it to you."

"I can fetch for myself," he mumbled, getting up.

She followed him through the door and stepped to his side, hurrying to match his long stride. Looking at him in the sunlight, she said brightly, "You've got dirt on your face."

He rubbed his knuckles against the powderstain on his forehead. The skin was tender, and just his touch prodded up the pain inside his skull. She hadn't one damned piece of an idea of the trouble she was stirring up here, he thought. She was a little kid with more spunk than sense. To her, this war was a fine, fancy game. She didn't understand things like pain and death at all. And it sure didn't look like he could explain to her.

With dim hope, he told himself in a day or two she'd get homesick and be glad to be taken back to her folks. Maybe.

CHAPTER 8

Logan took the men aside, one at a time, to get the story of the fight. Last of all, he hauled Brade into a quiet corner.

"You sure upset the buggy. What you trying to do, break up this outfit on me? I've been depending on you. You're *supposed* to be levelheaded and cool. You got a reputation for it. But I turn my back for a minute, and you go off like a hangfire. You gonna blow up in the middle of a raid like that, Lieutenant?"

"No, dammit! Look, Logan, I—it was a personal matter. A real personal one."

"The girl?"

"Yeah."

"She worth more to you than what we're trying to do for the state of Missouri?"

"She's—I just want her to get home where she belongs," Brade muttered.

"Well, Little Spring wants her here," Logan told him. "Boy says he wants to marry her."

"The hell!"

"He says if I send her away, he'll go after her. And Jake'll go with him. On top of that, the other men like her being here. They like her cooking, and they say she's got the right to stay if that's what *she* wants." Logan spread his hands as if he had the situation all mapped out on his palms for Brade to examine. "I don't want trouble among you men, dammit! I got a job to get done."

Brade eyed him. "Another raid?"

He nodded. "Town of Eastfork. You know it?"

"I been through it."

"Well, we've got to hit the bank there. I'm heading up tomorrow to take a look at things. I want you to go along with me."

"You want to get me away from here before I tangle with Jake or Little?"

"I'll own it's occurred to me. You and him are still both hot over this business. It won't hurt none for you to have a chance to cool down apart from each other."

Brade considered. Slowly, he said, "I ain't sure this is

gonna cool down. Springs and me been headed for trouble with each other. It ain't finished yet."

"If that's so, then you can damn well settle it between yourselves any way you want," Logan snapped. "I don't give a hoot in hell, long as you get it settled some way that won't stir up bad feelings among the rest of the men. We've got a job to do. That's what I'm concerned with. I got too good a deal with my friend in St. Louis to let you mess it up for me."

"Just who is this friend of yours in St. Louis?"

"That ain't anything *you* need to know."

"I'd *like* to know."

"Why?"

"There's things about this whole business that don't set too well with me."

Logan's gaze was narrow and probing. "What, for instance?"

"That fracas at Richmond. The way it turned into a shooting battle."

"That couldn't be helped."

"Maybe not, but I'd sure as hell hate to see something like that happen again. I don't like shooting at Missouri folk. Don't like it one damned bit. And I don't like the way Adam McCoy was making hay out of it in that speech of his," Brade told him.

"Ain't exactly fond of getting shot at that way myself," he muttered. "You got any suggestions?"

"Maybe we could change our way of working. S'pose we didn't ride in like bushwackers? S'pose we went in quiet and robbed the bank and lit out again before the townsfolk got into what was happening?"

"I dunno," Logan grumbled doubtfully.

"Might be we could do it without any danger to anybody," Brade went on. "Not any of them or us either. Our job's robbing, not killing, ain't it?"

Logan considered. He scowled and rubbed a hand at his face. As if he were thinking out loud, he said, "I reckon the important thing in Eastfork is showing that damned banker he either cooperates or gets all the trouble he's been promised . . ."

"Huh?"

"Nothing!" he snapped.

"What the hell you talking about?" Brade insisted.

Sighing, Logan answered, "That Eastfork banker's been talking the wrong way, making trouble for my friend in St. Louis. He's been warned to stop, and he ain't done it. We got to bust his bank to learn him his lesson."

"Do we have to kill anybody doing it?"

"Reckon not. Reckon it wouldn't hurt none to do it your way. Hell, I ain't exactly eager to get shot off my horse. All right, what say we ride in to Eastfork and look the place over and talk about it some more then. Leave in the morning?"

"That's fine with me," Brade said.

Traveling slow and easy, it took three days to reach Eastfork. It was a good-sized place, sitting astraddle of Miller's Creek, with a wooden bridge and a railroad trestle linking the two sides of it.

As they ambled their horses off the bridge, Logan pointed to a red brick building ahead. "That's a fair-looking hotel."

The sign on the front of it read *Union House,* and Brade saw several men in blue uniforms among the loafers on the porch. He eyed them warily and grumbled, "I s'pose it's no worse than any place else in town."

Logan grinned. "What's the matter? The soldiers?"

Brade only grunted in reply.

"You're a real hard-core Secesh, ain't you?"

"I'm hard-core against the Bluebellies taking this state away from them of us that live in it. Ain't you?"

"Yeah," Logan said. "Sure I am, but I wouldn't let it interfere with me getting a decent meal and bed. And the *name* of the place sure ain't gonna give you the itch."

They drew rein at the hitch rack in front of the hotel. Walking stiffly, trying not to limp, Brade followed Logan inside.

The room they got was a private one on the second floor. It was large and airy and, to Brade's notions, too expensive. But the husk mattress on the wide brass-framed bed felt fresh, and there were no signs of nits on the feather bed.

Brade pulled off his hat and studied his image in the big, clear mirror over the commode. Without the brim of the hat to shadow it, the powder mark on his forehead was obvious. He touched his fingers to it, trying to decide whether it was wearing away or not.

Gazing over Brade's shoulder at his own reflection, Logan said, "We got plenty of time before supper. I think I'll hunt up a barbershop and get slicked up."

"Go ahead. I'll hang around here."

"You could use shaving and shearing."

"Sure, and let some damned barber get curious why I got a gunpowder brand on my face. You just stop by that clerk and tell him I want some hot water."

Nodding, Logan began to whistle cheerily as he headed

out. Brade turned to the mirror again. Maybe that mark wouldn't draw as much attention as he feared, but he sure didn't fancy anyone in this town giving him enough notice to recognize him easy next time he came through. Couldn't wear his hat to the supper table, though. He tried brushing hair down over his forehead. Unkempt-looking, but it helped cover the mark.

The hot water was delivered, along with a towel and a fresh bar of soap. He latched the door behind the boy who'd brought them and began to strip. Bending his leg, he watched the way the scar on his thigh pulled as the muscles flexed.

It seemed like a man didn't necessarily die all at once. He could be killed off a piece at a time. A bullet tore a hole in his leg, then a chunk of the meat was burnt away with acid, and the leg never worked quite right for him again. A sudden gunshot too close took a subtle edge of his hearing away. He lost a war and surrendered a piece of his self-respect along with most of his rights as a citizen. Against his oath, he took up a gun and went to war again, and it turned out to be a business he couldn't find any pride in. A damned ugly business he only halfway understood, fighting under a commander without a name or face. He had a feeling this whole thing would set easier with him if only he knew more about the man in St. Louis.

When he'd finished dressing, he pulled on his coat, set the hat cocked forward to shadow his face, and went downstairs.

The sun was lowering, but the heat of day still hung in the dusty air. Only first beginnings of an evening breeze stirred across the porch. When he glanced at the loafers taking the air, he saw that one of them was reading a newspaper. The word *Rebels* showed in heavy black headline print.

As he walked over to get a better look, the man nodded sociably to him.

"What's that about the Rebs?" he asked, gesturing at the paper.

"Adam McCoy's still taking off at them bushwackers that raided Richmond," the man grinned, showing him the article. "Wants them all hunted down and lynched. They already strang up a couple of 'em, you know."

"No, I ain't heard." Brade managed to keep the surprise out of his face and voice. He knew damned well that *none* of the raiders had been caught.

"Sure! They got one feller right near to Richmond and stretched him where they found him. Couple days later, a posse took another'n up near Warrensburg. Nigh got a third over to Independence, but he shot his way out. Killed a little girl doing it. They'll get him, though. They know the names of eight of 'em. Got warrants out for 'em. Warrants, hell! I say lynch 'em all! So does Adam McCoy. Damned Rebs ain't none of 'em nothing but a bunch of murdering traitors. Ought to line 'em up and shoot 'em all. That'd larn 'em!"

"Reckon it would," Brade mumbled, gazing at the paper.

Citizens Up In Arms Against Rebels—Demand Retaliation For Richmond Massacre—Firmer Sanctions Against Traitors And Murderers—No Honest Man Safe From Depredations.

The item went on with a violent attack on the bushwackers in particular, the Secesh in general, and everyone who so much as tolerated a Reb sympathizer to live in his neighborhood. It called for *Honest Americans* to refuse to do business with the Rebs and sympathizers.

McCoy suggested legislation to enforce his proposals, saying it would drive the *traitors* out of the state and leave the land open for *Faithful Americans.* From there, he went to stumping for Drake, pointing out what he'd done in framing the new constitution. Then he finished off by saying that if he, himself, were in high office in Missouri, he'd see to it that all of these matters were properly attended to.

Despite the heat of the day, Brade felt a shiver along his spine as he read the piece. This was rotten business. The bank raids really seemed to be playing right into McCoy's hands. They were hefty grist for his mill, and he ground viciously. If he ever did get to be governor, the ex-Rebs who didn't leave the state would likely end up lynched. At best, they'd be damned bad off.

"Yeah, string 'em all up," the man with the paper was saying cheerfully.

One of the soldiers drifted over. He'd heard at least a part of the talk. He joined in, "Let *us* loose at 'em. If the government would send in us troops, we'd clean them out. I know how these bushwackers are. I fought 'em during the war. They're brave enough against women and children and crippled-up old Home Guard, but just let a few real soldiers get onto their tails, and they run like the devil."

Brade eyed him. "Where'd you fight bushwackers?"

"All over Missouri. Killed my share, too. Got the scalps to prove it."

"Lynch 'em, scalp 'em, burn 'em out! Get rid of 'em all!" the one with the paper chuckled. He looked at the soldier. "Reckon Adam McCoy wouldn't hold back of calling for Federal troops to help if he was governor."

"No sir! He'd put the state back under martial law. Let us sweep through 'em like a scythe. Every damned Reb in the state!"

"*All* the ex-Rebs?" Brade asked. "Not just the bushwackers?"

"They're all bushwackers at heart. The ones who ain't out doing robberies and murders are hiding and helping the ones who do it. I'll tell you, I'd issue another Order Eleven. Burn 'em out. I'd clean out Clay County and leave nothing but ashes . . ." Grinning, he went on describing the things he'd do.

Brade swallowed at the anger that burned in his throat and stared up the street, wishing to hell Logan would get back. He had a few things to talk about. The bank raids were stirring up too damned much hatred against the Rebs. He wanted *proof* that they were doing good as well.

The first bell for supper had already been rung when Logan finally arrived. There was no chance for serious talk at the common table. It wasn't till later that Brade managed to herd him up to the room and explain his feelings.

"I understand," Logan answered in a soft, soothing voice. "But you've been listening to a couple of hotheads and assuming that everybody's getting to think that way. You're wrong. And you're forgetting the power and influence my friend in St. Louis has."

"I ain't forgetting it. I'm asking you about it. I want to know who this man is and how he's getting good for us out of what we're doing."

"I *can't* tell you any more than you know now."

"Then you can damn well count me out of your rabble army!" Brade snapped. "I'm through with this whole business."

"*Now?* With us right on the edge of hitting this town? You're quitting on us?" Logan stared at him in accusation. "You're going to walk out on me right when I really *need* you?"

He nodded.

"Don't you understand how important this raid is, Lieutenant?" Logan persisted. "It's too late for me to replace you now, and I *can't* call off this raid. My friend in St. Louis has to stop this troublemaker here if he's gonna get hold of the political power he's after. You walk out on us now, and you're betraying us all. Don't you understand that!"

"I don't want to walk out, *if* this raid is really gonna do us some good. I just want *proof* that it will."

"Believe me, Brade, I swear it to you!" Logan said. "I wouldn't be chancing my own life if I didn't really believe I'd profit by it, would I?"

With a slow shake of his head, Brade muttered, "All right, I'll ride with you this one more time. But I want to *see* results afterward. When you take the plunder to this friend of yours, you bring back something from him to show me or tell me. Or else Eastfork is the last raid I make with you."

"That's agreeable," Logan sighed. He smiled. "I'm sure I can put an end to your worries for you. We've got to tend to this raid first, though."

They studied the bank the next day, going inside to change a bill and walking through the side streets near it. They drifted through most of that section of town afoot, getting the lay of the land and planning directions of escape. The day after that they spent riding the roads and trails around the town, discussing their plans. When it was all worked out, they headed back toward Dunkle's.

It would all be done quietly this time, the way Brade had suggested. There'd be no uniforms, no shouting and wild shooting. They'd just ride in, rob the bank, and ride out with the loot. It sounded perfect.

But Brade couldn't shake the sense of apprehension that rode his shoulders. He wasn't sure whether it was his concern over the right and wrong of the raids or some vague instinct, but he felt damned uneasy about the whole affair.

He hoped to hell he'd be able to talk Amy into going home before they left Dunkle's to make the raid.

CHAPTER 9

Logan had sent out the word. By the time he and Brade got back to Dunkle's, all but two of the men were there waiting. Those two had sent back replies that they'd had their fill of wild riding. Dunkle met Logan at the horse pen with that bit of news. Muttering together, they headed inside.

When he'd finished turning the horses into the pen, Brade followed. He found the card game had been relocated into the parlor. Most of the men had hands in it. A few others watched. But Jake and Little Spring sat together on the sofa, paying it no attention. As Brade walked in, their eyes fixed on him.

Logan was standing by the chimney with one foot up on a firedog and a cup in his hand. He sipped at his coffee, nodded to Brade, and announced, "I reckon we're all here now. Leastways, all of us that's coming."

The game stopped. The men looked expectantly toward

him. All except Jake and Little. They both kept watching Brade darkly.

From the corner of his eye, he studied on them. Little was still pale and sickly. The bandages wrapped around his chest lumped under his shirt. He had both of his revolvers stuck into his belt, but he didn't look strong enough to use them.

Logan began talking. He was sketching out the plan they'd worked up for Eastfork. Brade knew it already. His attention wandered. He avoided looking directly at the Springs, but he could feel their eyes steady on him. He could feel the hatred. He could smell it, like the harsh dusty scent that sometimes came before a storm.

Logan's talk took a while. There was a lot for him to say, and there were questions when he was done. But none of them came from Jake or Little. Brade had a notion neither one of them had paid much attention to the plan.

He was very aware of the two Colt revolvers in his own belt. Both were clean and loaded. The coat wasn't buttoned. One gun butt edged from under it. Thinking of the guns, Brade felt his right hand flex slightly. He wondered how the Springs meant to attack. With some warning, or from behind?

"Well, that's it," Logan said finally. Brade started to turn away then.

"Bradenton!" Little Spring hollered.

Brade wheeled, his hand halfway to the revolver. He stopped it before his fingers touched, jerking it back to his side. Jumpy as hell, he thought.

Little was on his feet, standing with his legs apart and his shoulders hunched. His eyes were vicious, eager, but his right hand was caught in his brother's tight grip.

Hanging onto the kid, trying to pull him down onto the sofa again, Jake snapped, "Shut up and sit down!"

Little wavered uncertainly. He didn't want to obey, but Jake was boss in the family. Reluctantly, looking like he hated himself for it, he eased down.

For an instant, Brade felt relief. But it was gone as suddenly as lightning. He knew there'd be no trouble with Little —but because Jake intended to handle it all himself.

It all showed in Jake's eyes as he stood up. Facing Brade, he said, "Satisfaction, *Lieutenant* Bradenton! You give us the insult, g'damn you! You give us worse than any damn *insult,* and I got a damn right to kill you like a wild hog. Only I ain't gonna. G'damn bushwacker taking on to be a officer and a gentleman—I show you *gentleman!* I'm calling you to face me like a *gentleman*. You got the gut for it?"

Brade stared at him coldly, studying the challenge. Slowly,

he answered, "One wild hog against another, according to gentlemen's rules? Sounds fair to me."

"G'damn you, *now!*" Jake hollered.

"Hold on!" Logan waved a hand at Jake. "You just said *by the rules.*"

Jake struggled back his anger. He looked questioningly at the men who watched. Their faces showed excited curiosity. They spoke up in agreement with Logan. One of them said, "You got to have seconds."

Turning toward Collis, Brade said softly, "Coll, I'd be obliged if you'd talk for me."

"I never done it before. I ain't sure of the rules."

"Hell, nobody here is. There ain't a real gentleman in the bunch of us. You just set it up with Jake's man, make sure it's fair to both of us."

Collis nodded in agreement.

Jake's first glance had been toward his brother, but evidently he remembered a man wasn't supposed to have close kin for a second. He looked around, settling his gaze on Logan. "Captain, will you talk for me?"

"I ain't sure it'd be right," Logan said.

"I'd accept it," Brade put in. "I'd be damned glad of it."

With a sigh, Logan said, "All right, who's talking for you?"

"Collis."

"Come on, Coll. Let's get the jawing part done before they bust loose and forget they're both *gentlemen.*" As he headed toward the doorway, he shot a glance back at Brade and at Jake. "You two stay the hell away from each other till whatever time we set. You understand?"

Jake sunk down onto the sofa and whispered something to Little. The kid began talking back to him. It looked like Little was arguing that the insult was against *him.* But Jake was holding firm.

Brade ducked out of the house and headed for the horse pen. Leaning on the rails, he waited, knowing that Collis would hunt him up once it was all settled.

Half the night seemed to have dragged by before Collis finally came. He walked up, leaned on the rails at Brade's side, and said, "Sun up, day after tomorrow. That suit you?"

"Sooner the better. I'd as leave it was tomorrow."

"Day after's soon enough. We got a kind of a problem about weapons though. Logan knows some about these things, and he says they're supposed to be smoothbore flintlocks, but we got none of that kind around here. Should be the arms are a real close match, but we ain't sure how to arrange that either."

"There's matched pairs of revolvers around," Brade suggested. "My Colts are a pretty good match to each other."

"Sure, only you're used to them, but Jake's used to that French thing he carries. Wouldn't be fair to him to give you both Colt revolvers. Or Remingtons, either. They're a lot more like Colts than like that LeMat."

"What do you want to do?"

"We talked it out a bit. Decided to put it to you fellers if you'd as soon just use your regular handguns and figure it's a fair match. Us seconds will do the loading. One round for each of you, with a half charge of powder. You be agreeable to that?"

"Sure," Brade grunted. He grinned slightly and added, "Long as it ain't the buckshot barrel on the French pistol that Jake loads."

"Hell, no." Collis returned the grin feebly. He fell thoughtfully silent for a moment, then said, "You don't seem much bothered by the notion of facing him this way."

"Should I be?"

"*I* would."

"I can't say I'm exactly happy about it. But I'd sooner have it this way than have him stalking my back."

"He might kill you."

"I ain't much afraid of that. I could get just as killed robbing a bank."

"Might be you'll kill him."

"I won't be in mourning long for him if I do," Brade muttered.

Collis sighed. "Hell, I'm supposed to try talking you out of this duel."

"You're supposed to try talking *Jake* out of it. I'm the one who's challenged. Way I understand it, I'm supposed to go along with whatever everybody else decides."

"*I* decided you're a pair of damn fools."

"Reckon I can go along with that all right. It ain't gonna stop us fighting, though."

"No," he agreed.

Brade asked him, "Anything else I should know?"

"Dueling's against the law," he muttered.

"Hell!" Brade gave a snorting laugh, "So's being a second in one. So's robbing banks."

"Then far as you're concerned, it's set?"

"Yeah."

Collis leaned silently on the rails a while longer. He spoke up again suddenly. "Brade, what about Amy Potter?"

"What about her?"

"She's in love with you."

"She *thinks* she is."

"She's a right nice girl."

"She's a damn-fool baby!" Brade snapped. Even in the darkness, he was aware of Collis' questioning glance. He swallowed at the surge of anger and said quietly, "Look, Coll, she's got no business hanging around here. If I—if this damned duel goes wrong on me, try to talk her into going back home, will you?"

"Sure, only . . ."

"Only what?"

"Only—oh hell, Brade, don't let it go wrong!"

"I don't intend to," he answered. It seemed as if Collis were worse worried about this business than he was. But then, Collis had a wife and kids waiting for him, he thought. Likely that made a difference to a man.

"Coll, why don't you quit this bunch?" he said. "Why don't you go back home to your family where you belong?"

There was an edge of sadness in Collis' voice. "One of these days, I will."

Brade shivered slightly. He wasn't sure whether it was from a touch of coolness in the night breeze or because of that feeling of apprehension—of wrongness—that prickled along his spine.

The sun was a hazy reddish disc barely clear of the treetops. It hadn't yet lifted the mists that lay in the hollows. Dew lay heavy on the grass and brush. It darkened the leaves of the trees. Somewhere in the distance, a flicker cracked the stillness with a complaint about the morning. Its voice seemed muffled by the mists.

Collis moved his lips slightly, silently counting the paces he measured off. Walking beside him, Brade matched his stride. Twelve paces. Logan and Jake Spring were measuring another twelve in the other direction.

Halting, Collis used the heel of his boot to gouge a line in the dirt. Brade glanced back at Logan and Jake. The road here was straight, almost level, with no shadows falling across it. A clear field. The light was weak, though, and the breeze ragged. Too gusty. With a half charge of powder in the pistol, Brade judged Jake would be an adequate target but not a good one.

He was used to firing half charges. It was a habit he'd picked up during the war. For close-up shooting, mostly off the back of a horse, a half charge was fine. The pistol held steadier, not kicking so hard or throwing as much smoke, and a man got twice as many shots from a flask of powder. Close up, it was better than a full load. But at a distance, the ball lost punch and accuracy.

As he took his place on the score, Collis asked, "How you feel?"

"Hungry."

"It wouldn't be good to stuff your gut before business like this."

Brade grinned slightly. "I've fought hungry often enough. Don't recall we ever had to shoot our way up from a supper table."

He took a quick look at the men bunched along the side of the road. Amy was with them. She stood with Little Spring, clutching his arm.

Brade knew she'd tried to see him yesterday. He figured she had wanted to talk him out of this duel, so he'd made a point of keeping away from her. He hadn't wanted to argue or try explaining. And he hadn't been too sure he wouldn't give in, if she pressed him hard enough.

He told himself again that this wasn't just a matter of pride. It was the lancing of a sore that would fester otherwise. Jake had a grudge that he'd carry and nurse if it didn't end on this field. Jake was dangerous enough now. He'd be a lot worse if he was let to brood any longer.

And Brade wanted desperately to get it over with. Yesterday had been a damned long, tight-strung day. This morning he felt calm. But it was the carefully balanced calm, edged with a fine wildness, that came when a long wait finally broke into action.

He grinned at the taut set of Collis' face. "You look worried."

"I am," Collis owned. He touched his fingers to the butts of the two revolvers in his belt. Drawing one—Brade's—he said, "You understand you're not to raise this thing until Logan says *fire*. Then, you can snap shoot or take your time or whatever you want."

"Yeah." Brade held out his left hand. They knew this bit of the ritual. Collis put the barrel of the revolver into his palm. He closed his fingers over it.

"You understand Logan and me each got a loaded pistol," Collis continued. "If you fire before he gives the word, one of us will shoot you down."

Brade nodded.

"You only got one round in there. Don't forget that."

"I won't." he grinned again. "Don't be so damned nervous. Nobody's going to be shooting at *you*."

Collis grunted. With a sigh, he said, "Stand firm." Turning, he headed to meet Logan. Together, they walked off the road.

Brade stood with the revolver in his hand hanging muzzle down. There was dampness on his palm. He wondered if it was dew or sweat. The mist was thick. It beaded on his lashes. He blinked, then rubbed the back of his left wrist across his eyes.

Jake was standing with his right side toward Brade, offering as small a target as he could. His coat hung loose, the bulk of it disguising the exact position of his body.

Brade's stance was the same. His own coat was unbuttoned, the collar turned up. It prodded slightly at the edge of his jaw as he looked across his shoulder at Jake. The tug of the sleeve when he raised his arm wouldn't bother him. He was used to wearing a coat or jacket of some kind into action.

His thumb touched the cocked hammer of the revolver lightly. His forefinger lay gently against the trigger. He studied Jake, judging the exact move his arm would have to make bringing the gun up to align the sights between his eye and Jake's body.

He wondered what the hell was taking Logan so long.

Jake looked steady and solid. Brade couldn't see any trace of fear or fidgeting in him. Just steady determination.

"Ready?" Logan called.

The dew was beading on Brade's lashes again. He tried to ignore it.

"Fire!"

His hand rose. Over the sights, he saw Jake's arm outstretched, pointing toward him. He saw the puff of smoke from the LeMat through sudden white haze from his own revolver. The shots sounded together, one rolling into the other like thunder. He wasn't sure who'd fired first.

He had felt no impact. Grinning slightly, he looked across the sights. Jake stared back at him. The gusty breeze swirled away the screen of powdersmoke between them.

Brade let the hand holding the empty pistol drop to his side.

"Stand firm!" Logan called. He and Collis walked toward Jake. The men bunched by the roadside muttered together, their voices soft with restraint.

Logan and Collis were talking with Jake. They spoke too low for Brade to catch the words. But he could see Jake shaking his head insistently. The seconds were dutifully trying to talk him out of carrying this any further. But he was maintaining that his quarrel was far from satisfied. Brade knew it'd take more than one bloodless round to satisfy Jake.

While he waited, he was thinking through the shot he'd fired. He thought the ball had gone to the left and low. His own fault, or had Collis shortloaded? He saw Logan take the LeMat out of Jake's hand. Collis came toward him to get the Colt.

"He ain't gonna settle for less than blood," he told Brade as he took the gun.

"Might be his own," Brade muttered.

"I don't like this business. Not at all," Collis said. He went back to Logan. Together, they reloaded the weapons and then returned them to the principals.

"Ready?" Logan called.

Brade watched Jake.

"Fire!"

The revolver rose. The hammer notch and muzzle pin aligned, higher and to the right this time. Across them he saw the LeMat spit smoke. He heard its roar and something plucked at the back of his coat. At the same instant, he saw a small puff of smoke from under the hammer of his own revolver. The crack of the cap was a sharp, thin sound against the echo of the LeMat. But there was no thud of the gun butt into his hand, no blast of powder slamming a ball through the muzzle.

"Misfire!" he hollered.

"Stand firm," Logan answered, starting toward him.

He waited, thinking about that tug against his back. There wasn't any pain or numbness. He didn't think he'd been hit.

Logan held out a hand for the revolver. Giving it to him, Brade turned to Collins. "Coll, take a look at my back."

"You ain't hit?" Logan asked, squinting at him.

Collis stepped behind him. Thinly, he said, "You got a hole in your coat."

"Hold on a minute." Brade shrugged the coat down his shoulders. He couldn't feel anything wrong, but he knew that sometimes the excitment could deaden pain.

"Ticked your coat all right," Collis told him. "Didn't touch your shirt, though."

"Dammit," he muttered. It was a sigh of relief.

"You steady enough to go again?" Logan asked him.

"Sure."

"You don't get no free round. Misfire counts same as a shot."

He shrugged and settled the coat on his shoulders again. "Just check my powder, will you? See that it's dry."

Collis nodded.

"What the hell's the matter? Did I get him?" Jake called.

Logan hollered back, "No. Did he get you?"

"With a misfire?" Jake laughed. But he didn't really sound amused. It was beginning to wear at his nerves, Brade thought. He knew it was wearing at his own. He still felt the taut calm, but a vague uneasiness had begun in his gut.

Logan and Collis took the revolvers to reload. Jake stretched and yawned. Grinning—or smirking—he called to Brade, "I reckon I got your range now, *Lieutenant, sir.*"

Brade grinned back at him.

Collis brought over the loaded revolver. As he put it into Brade's hand, he said hoarsely, "Finish it this round, dammit! I can't take much more of this."

"All right. I'll try."

"Ain't you been trying?"

"What the hell you think?"

Mumbling something under his breath, Collis turned to rejoin Logan.

"Ready?"

Brade felt a muscle twitch where his shoulder joined his neck. He knew exactly how Collis felt. Standing in the middle of a battle was one thing. All this damned waiting around was something else. It could sure weary a man. He wondered if that was the reason for the ritual of dueling. Maybe folks figured after a couple of rounds like this, a man could find it a damnsight easier to forgive an insult. If he'd thought Jake would really back down, he'd have been glad to do it himself.

"Fire!"

As the sights came together, his finger was closing. The hammer dropped, striking thunder. In its echo, he heard the scream.

It wasn't Jake who'd screamed. That was Little Spring's voice.

Through the flung smoke that stung at his eyes, Brade saw Jake flinch. He saw the LeMat spit with its muzzle too far down. The ball plowed dirt, throwing it up wildly from the deep furrow.

Jake staggered back, his mouth open. No sound came from it. He dropped to his knees. Stretching out one hand, he lowered himself to the ground. He seemed to move with a quiet deliberation, like a man settling down to rest a while. He didn't look hurt at all—except for the blood spewing from his throat in pulsing spurts.

"Stand firm! Stand firm!" Logan was hollering as he ran toward Jake.

Brade stood, the revolver at his side. It felt uncommon heavy. His fingers wanted to open and let it drop. He watched Jake stretch out like he meant to take a lazy nap. The man moved with a terrible slowness.

Suddenly, his back heaved with a shuddering breath. The LeMat was still in his hand. He seemed to be trying to lift it. Then, he was lost from Brade's sight, blocked by the crowd that surrounded him.

Brade could hear Little Spring's gulping, soblike breaths. He saw Amy there, still holding the boy's arm. She had no damned business watching something like this, he thought angrily.

Pushing through between the men, she let go Little's arm and went to her knees beside Jake. Logan and Collis were bending over him, too. It was Collis who got up and started toward Brade.

"How the hell long am I supposed to just stand here?" Brade asked him.

"Don't reckon it matters now," he said dully.

Brade stuck the revolver into his belt and headed toward Jake. The men had turned him onto his back. Amy'd pulled off her apron, and Logan was trying to stop the bleeding by stuffing it against the hole in Jake's neck. It didn't seem to be doing any good.

Jake's chest rose in shallow, hurried jerks. Suddenly, his whole body trembled. And then, he lay still. The blood stopped spurting. It came in a small, thin trickle.

"He's dead." Logan looked up. His eyes found Brade. "A fair fight. He knew what could happen. It's done now."

"No, it ain't!" Little hollered, his voice high and wavering. "It *ain't* done, goddammit!"

Logan got stiffly to his feet. He sighed, a sound that could have been weariness or disgust. "For now it is. We've got business to tend to. I ain't wasting any more men this way till it's over. Little, if you figure you've got a fight, you keep the lid on it, you hear me? Anything you want to settle, you hold onto it till we've come back from Eastfork."

"He killed my brother," Little said intensely.

Logan gazed at the boy through eyes that were hot coals. "I said no more trouble till after Eastfork. You hear me?"

The boy didn't answer.

Brade realized that Amy was staring at him. He glanced toward her. She was shaking her head as if she could deny that all of this had happened.

He felt accused. This wasn't *his* doing, he told himself. He'd been challenged, and there hadn't been anything else he could do. He'd had to fight—shoot Jake or be shot.

Logan looked at him in question.

"I'm done with it," he muttered, wiping his hand against

his thigh. He could still feel the impression of the gun butt on his palm. It wouldn't wipe off. As he walked away, he was aware of the ache in his leg. He was limping again, and he couldn't help it.

CHAPTER 10

The kitchen was deserted, the hearth cold. The coffeepot was empty and clean. Jerking open the safe, Brade hunted out Dunkle's jug. He poured himself a cup of corn doublings and went out through the back door.

The lifting sun had begun to raise the dew at last. The moist air threatened a hot day, once the sun got high. He could feel sweat trickling down his sides as he climbed the bluff. From the ledge, he could see the men carrying Jake's body into the house.

The brush was thick and lush around the creek that fed the sluice, but he found a small clearing at its edge a ways back. He settled there on a windfallen log. His face itched. Shoving back the straggling hair, he wiped at his forehead with the back of his hand. It wasn't just the day's warmth that had him sweating, he thought. He took a deep swallow of the whiskey.

Something crackled in the brush behind him.

Breath held, he listened. Someone had followed him. As he looked over his shoulder, Amy's voice came to him.

"Brade?"

He didn't want to face her. But he was afraid he couldn't escape her this time. He called back, "Yeah?"

She came to his side, clutching her skirts. Her knuckles were white, her face pale and drawn. Probing at him with her gaze, she said, "You killed Jake Spring."

Her voice was so flat and toneless that he wasn't at all sure how she meant it. Just a statement of fact, or an accusation?

He sipped at the whiskey, holding it in his mouth. Words tumbled through his mind. Words about how it had come to the point where either he or Jake had to die, or at least to be hurt bad. Words about chance and luck and a man's honor. But he didn't speak them. Swallowing the whiskey, he nodded.

"Now Little says that he's going to kill you."

There was still no reading her meaning from her tone. He

watched her from the corner of his eye, waiting, wishing he could run from her.

She paused as if she expected an answer from him. But he didn't know what her question was.

After a moment, she gave a small shake of her head. She seemed to be trying to brush away some dark thought. Reaching toward him, she touched her fingertips lightly to his forehead. "You've got dirt on your face."

"It ain't dirt. It's gunpowder. Under the skin. It'll wear away in time."

"Will it?"

"Yeah."

Her touch was warm, moist against his face. He pulled away from it.

Smoothing her skirts, she seated herself on the log beside him. She was still waiting. He could feel it—her tension and his own. Suddenly, he thought that whatever her question might be, it wasn't for *him*. It was something she had to answer to herself.

She looked at the cup in his hand. "Is that whiskey?"

"Yeah." He wondered if she wanted some of it. She'd never taken a drink that he knew of. It wouldn't be proper for a lady to take strong drink. Especially not for a little girl like Amy. But maybe there were times when even a little girl could use the comfort that came out of a jug. He wondered if he ought to offer her a swallow.

Glancing sidewise at her, it occurred to him that she wasn't such a little girl as he figured. It was as if suddenly, when he wasn't looking, she'd begun to grow up. Not in a way that he could see outright, but in some way that he sensed unclearly.

"Brade, this bushwacking, this war with the charcoal radicals, you can't ever really win it, can you?"

"We can give 'em a hard time, maybe keep Drake out of the Senate and McCoy out of the State House."

"But you can't come to terms and make peace with them. They won't ever take your parole and let you go home again, will they?"

"I can go home," he muttered.

She didn't believe him. With a slow shake of her head, she said, "You're into it too deep to ever get out."

"Nobody knows me," he snapped. "Ain't nobody we've raided ever seen my face. Ain't nobody could witness against me." He felt like squirming under her gaze. He took a long swallow of the whiskey.

"But you couldn't go home and be really safe there, ever again. And now you're in trouble here, too. Now Little Spring means to kill you."

"He won't do it."

She looked deep into her own thoughts. From far away, she said, "You didn't want to fight Jake, did you? *I* caused it by coming here."

He looked at her. A tear hung on her lash. It broke loose to trickle down her cheek.

"Hey, don't do that!" He brushed at it with his knuckles, as if she were just a little girl. It left a damp, shiny streak. Another one began to grow on the lash.

"You could go away. Somewhere far away, outside of the States, where nobody'd know you."

"That's the one thing I can't do," he answered.

"But—"

"*I*'d know me, Amy. I might get away from Little Spring and from the law and anybody who'd name me for a raider, but I'd never get away from myself."

She met his eyes. Snuffling, she fought the tears. "Is it too late for *me,* Brade? If—if—could I stop the trouble with Little? If I went home now?"

He almost told her the truth. But he held back of it. Instead, he said, "It's not too late. Will you go home?"

She nodded.

There was nothing of the little girl in her face. Nothing teasing or pouting or playful about her. The eyes that looked into his had a seriousness and depth he'd never seen there before.

He felt twisted inside. His hands wanted to touch her, to hold onto her. He wanted to protect and comfort her. And to keep her there beside him.

"Will you take me home, Brade?"

"Yeah," he said. He gulped down what was left of the whiskey.

"Will you promise not to fight Little?"

"I'll do every damned thing I can to keep from it." He gazed at her, studying a new thought. It wasn't one he liked, but maybe it was a good one. "You really like him, don't you?"

"Yes."

"A lot?"

She nodded, her eyes questioning.

"Maybe you like him enough that he'd make you a good husband?"

"What do you mean, Brade?"

"He's just a wild kid now, but maybe it ain't too late for him to tame down and settle. If somebody took him in hand and gave him reason enough to try. He could get some sense into his head before it's too late for him. You might give him reason to learn better, Amy. He's in love with you."

"But I love *you,*" she protested.

"Like hell! You loved George Todd the same way—"

"No!"

"Yes. You weren't but a little girl all full of admiring a bunch of show-off fellers with brassbound revolvers in their belts. You got took with the fancy talk of wild riding. Little boys get a notion they're going to grow up to be pirates or knights or Robin Hood or some such. Only you being a girl, you got a notion to be in love with a pirate or Robin Hood. That's just a little girl notion. I guess I'm a pirate all right, but you're old enough to get shed of such little girl notions. You start looking for a man who'll make you a husband instead of hunting for something out of story tales."

"No," she said again, more softly this time, but just as intently.

"Look here, Amy, suppose I wasn't around, suppose I'd got killed in the war, or went off somewhere else, or had a wife already—suppose you knew damned well I wasn't coming back—then how would you feel about Little Spring to court you?"

"But Brade—"

"I said *suppose*. You give me an answer."

"I guess so," she mumbled.

He wasn't sure whether she might mean it or was just saying it to satisfy him. He asked, "Would you let him court you? Just give him a fair chance before you get your mind all made up?"

She sighed, "I suppose."

"Will you promise me that? Just promise me you'll give him a chance?"

She nodded reluctantly.

"Say it."

"I promise."

"All right." He got to his feet. She held her hand toward him. As he took it, her fingers wrapped tight around his, clinging to him. She faced him. He had a god-awful urge to slide his arms around her, to kiss her, just this once.

He said, "I think we'd best leave after dark. Keep it quiet. Best none of the men find out you're leaving till after you've gone."

She nodded, waiting.

He led her down the bluff. Leaving her in the yard, he headed across the road. Collis and Archer were under the clump of elms, digging.

Wordlessly, Brade took the shovel from Collis and jabbed

it into the earth. He dug fiercely, as if he meant to bury more in the hole than just the body of Jake Spring. He dug with a violence that washed him with sweat and aggravated the ache in his leg.

Neither Archer nor Collis spoke. He was glad of it. There was nothing to say, no way to explain himself.

Logan had wanted to dump Jake's body into the hole like the carcass of a dead horse, but Little Spring had been bad upset at the idea. The men sided with Little. A couple of them tore planks off an old outshed to put together a box. They laid Jake out decent, nailed on the lid, and brought the box to the hole.

Goforth's family followed preaching. He knew the words. Too damned many of them, as far as Brade was concerned. Waiting at the graveside was worse than standing on the field had been. Goforth droned on and on in a soft mumble while the sun reached down to wrap them all in its stifling heat. It brought sweat and flies that droned as if they mocked the preaching.

Logan interrupted suddenly. "G'dammit, he's dead! Let's get him put away befoie he begins to stink!"

Whatever Little started to holler, Archer's big hand on his shoulder stopped him. Goforth swallowed hard and muttered, "Amen." Dunkle muffled a chuckle. Shooting him a glance of disapproval, Collis bent to pick up the shovel.

Brade wondered if he ought to take a hand in filling the grave. But Little was still standing there, staring at the clods Collis dropped onto the box. And suddenly, Brade wanted worse than anything else to get the hell away from it all. Wheeling, he stalked toward the house.

He heard Amy's light footsteps following him. He didn't let her catch up, though. He went on inside, not stopping until he'd reached the kitchen.

"Brade?" she called, "Please wait."

He turned as she came through the doorway. "You want to cook a meal?" he asked sharply to stop her of whatever she might intend to say. "If you want, I'll lay a fire for you."

She studied him a silent moment, then nodded as if she understood. Wiping her hands, she began to set out the things she'd need.

Once he got the fire going, he meant to head on outside where he could be alone. But he realized that he didn't want to be alone. Only, he didn't want company either. Uncertain, he looked at Amy.

She'd set in to snapping beans. She sat on the bench with the bowl in her lap. Her fingers darted as if they were dancing.

Slender fingers that could be delicate in their touch. Warm fingers that he knew could trace fox fire across his cheek and twist knots inside him.

Without looking up, she said, "Would you please put the coffeepot on, Brade?"

He did it. Then, he sat down across the table from her, sensing that she wasn't going to say a wrong thing. She understood that he didn't want talk. And her silent presence was oddly comforting.

Watching her hands, he pondered on it. He'd known her all his life, but suddenly he didn't know her. He'd known a little girl, and this was a woman. Those gentle fingers could brush away troubled thoughts. Her nearness could comfort pain.

He told himself that she deserved a damnsight better than widow's weeds.

When supper was done, the men picked up their card game in the parlor. And Brade went to the horse pen to saddle up.

Amy met him there, carrying the little bundle of belongings she'd brought with her. He helped her onto the horse. As she settled astride, her skirts caught up, showing her ankles.

"Next time you get a man to steal a mount for you, have him fetch you a *woman's* saddle," he grunted.

She made no answer, but tugged at the skirt trying to make it fall lower.

He knew he'd spoken too harshly and he'd hurt her. It was just as well, he told himself. She might be turning woman, but she still had foolish little girl notions that she'd be better off without.

Stepping up onto the bay, he led her toward the road. The moonlight was bright enough to satisfy his horse. It was used to traveling at night. But Amy's filly wasn't. It took shy and skitterish, slowing their pace. After they'd traveled a ways, Brade traded horses. It took him some work and attention to keep the mare in hand, but he was glad for something to concentrate on. Fighting the horse was easier than facing his own thoughts.

He was weary, sitting off side in the saddle to favor his aching leg, when they topped the rise and saw Potter's farm ahead. The sun was a white fire on the horizon, washing the fields in pale light and stretching long thin shadows behind the house and buildings. Smoke from the chimney told him that the Potters were awake and around.

Drawing rein, he said, "Change horses again. You can go the rest of the way by yourself."

"Aren't you coming in?" she asked.

"No."

"Don't you want to rest a while?" She looked at him with concern, as if she could read his weariness.

He straightened in the saddle, then stepped down. It felt good to unkink. He wished he could go on to the house with her, maybe set in the kitchen and sip coffee for a while, maybe curl up in the barn and sleep. But he didn't dare. He didn't want to face her folks. And if he stopped here—he was afraid he might not leave again.

He said sullenly, "It wasn't *my* doing that you ran away. I don't mean to be tongue-whipped for it."

"They'll tongue-whip *me,*" she muttered.

"Running away was your idea. You deserve it."

The way she looked at him gave him a feeling that he was likely to do anything she asked. Drawing a deep breath, he straightened his shoulders and tightened his grip on his determination. He told himself he *couldn't* give in to her. There were too many debts. He'd promised Logan he'd stick through the raid on Eastfork. He owed that to the state of Missouri. He owed himself to find the men who'd burned his farm. He had to hunt down the pale-eyed Orin Coleman.

"No, dammit! I'm not taking *your* whipping for you. Understand?" he snapped at her.

She nodded submissively.

He held his hands to her. She slid down off the horse into his arms. Suddenly, he was holding her close, his mouth on hers. For a moment—

He jerked away, frightened by his own feelings. He was too damned close to surrendering and staying. Only, he knew he couldn't settle and live at peace with himself unless he respected himself. And he couldn't do that if he left promises broken and debts unpaid.

"You *have* to go back?" she asked.

"Yeah."

"But you'll come home again?"

"No. I'm not coming back." He had to make her believe that, or else she might wait. He couldn't let her wait for him.

"You will," she said.

"No!"

"You've got land here."

"I'll sell it and go to Texas. But I *won't* be coming back here." He stepped up onto the bay and wheeled it away from her.

"I'll be waiting for you, Brade!" she called after him.

He made no answer, but flung the horse into a hard run. He rode as if he were being chased.

Swinging wide across his own land, he passed by the weather-worn ruins of the buildings and through the fields that were sprung high with weeds. Damned good land going to waste, he thought as he paused at the edge of the woods to look back. Even in weeds, it yielded a fine, lush crop.

The old oak by the gate was silhouetted against the morning sky. He'd cut down the noose the night he'd found it there, but the memory was still vivid. He could almost smell the hot char and wisps of smoke that had risen from the ashes of the house.

Someone had to pay for that, he told himself. He'd finish the Eastfork business with Logan and then quit. Leave the bushwackers with their damned mysterious war and go tend to his own private war. Finish what he'd begun.

He turned away and gigged the horse into the forest, knowing he'd never farm this land again.

CHAPTER 11

Brade slept through the heat of the day in the brush and rode on after sunset. It was well into morning when he reached Dunkle's farm again. And Little Spring was gone.

According to Collis, the kid had left as soon as he found out that Brade and Amy were gone. He'd left cursing, swearing to kill Brade and have the girl for his wife. It was better than Brade had hoped for.

He'd expected trouble. He'd been afraid it would take force to set Little out after Amy. But luck seemed to be running with him. If it held, the boy would go to Potter's. In keeping with her promise, Amy'd stay put there and let the boy court her. He'd hang around close by, away from the bushwackers and out of trouble. Even if she decided Little wasn't the man for her, she'd have got a taste of courting, maybe got shed of her damn-fool ideas about Brade. At least, that was his hope.

Logan wasn't sorry to be rid of the boy either. He had a feeling that Little wouldn't have been steady enough to do any good without Jake to hold rein on him. Since Ril and Gargan had quit, it only left eight men to ride to Eastfork. But the way the raid was planned, eight would be enough.

They traveled by twos and threes and came together in the woods south of the town for one last meeting. It had rained during the night. They hunkered in the misty dawn, checking their revolvers, swatting mosquitoes, and going over their plan once more. Then they mounted up and rode out by twos and threes. Brade and Collis were the last to leave.

Slouch hats shadowed their faces and linen dusters covered the guns in their belts. They kept to an easy pace, chatting together like men headed into town on common business. A mule skinner who drove past on the coach road barely gave them a glance.

The mists were risen, the sun bright, when they crossed the plank bridge in the middle of town. Here the coach road was cobbled and named Mill Street. It was lined with tall stone and brick buildings, homes with polished brass doorknobs and clipped lawns, businesses with plate glass windows and bright-painted signs.

"That's the bank up ahead." Brade nodded toward a huge two-storied building of dressed limestone. It looked as unyielding as an armory. On the Mill Street side, it housed a dry goods merchant and a grocer. The bank entrance was on Clennon, the cross street. From where they were, Brade and Collis couldn't see the doorway yet. But they spotted the three men at the hitch rack on the corner who were to watch it.

Dunkle, Beès, and Archer studied on Dunkle's horse as if they were bargaining a sale or trade. They seemed intent on it, though Brade caught Dunkle's quick glance in his direction.

A wagon rattled out of Clennon Street, turning into Mill. Brade and Collis paused to let it pass. Waiting, Brade scanned the buildings along the street. The hardware store at his left, on the corner across from the bank, caught his eye. There was a spang new Henry repeating rifle on display in the window. He thought as how a farmer needed a good rifle or shotgun just as much as a bank robber needed a handy brace of revolvers. Once he'd done with the bank-robbing business and tended to the jayhawkers who'd burnt his farm, he'd settle down again. He'd get himself one of those Henry repeaters then. Not that one, though. When his business in Eastfork was finished, he didn't plan on coming back again.

A boy of seventeen or so stopped to stare at the Henry. The wagon rolled past. Lifting rein, Brade and Collis turned their horses onto Clennon Street.

A narrow alley separated the hardware store from a small café. Next to it, a drugstore displayed oddities in glass jars in its windows. Two men were standing with their backs to the street, looking into the window—or at the reflections in the glass. Holgram and Goforth were ready.

Swinging the bay in at the hitch rail directly in front of the bank, Brade gave a quick look to the man leaning against the wall of the building, intent on his whittling. Logan was ready, too.

Holgram and Goforth had begun drifting along the walk toward the bank. Logan kept busy peeling chips. Unless something went wrong, he'd stay right where he was until everyone else was mounted up and moving again.

Brade stepped off the horse. As he gave the reins a loop over the rail, he scanned the other people on the street. A couple strolled along, their arms linked. Two men deep in conversation were ambling in the other direction. A fellow in buttonless Confederate gray with one empty sleeve pinned up hurried past. In the distance, a couple of kids were tossing a ball back and forth. A young dandy on a high-stepping black crossed the street. A buggy turned in from Mill at a slow trot, rolling on by. All in all, peaceful and quiet. Just the way a street should be in the morning of a very ordinary day.

Then why the hell did he have that icy feeling of being watched, he asked himself. It shivered unpleasantly along his spine, not a vague apprehensiveness but a downright strong feeling of being stared at.

With Collins at his side, he walked into the bank.

There was a well-dressed side-whiskered old gentleman at the teller's window, seeming in casual conversation with the man behind it. They spoke in soft tones, smiling and nodding at each other like old friends.

No one was at the cashier's place, but two men were behind the low wooden fence that divided the room. One was leaning across it, talking to a man and woman who looked like farm folk. They didn't seem very happy about whatever he was saying. The other sat at a desk, bent over some kind of paperwork. He gave Brade and Collis a quick glance as they stepped in, dipped his pen, and went back to his figuring.

Just inside the doorway, Brade turned toward Collis. The door opened again. Holgram and Goforth walked in, stopped, and looked around.

Side-whiskers realized he was taking up the teller's time. With an apologetic smile to the newcomers, he cut short his conversation and headed out.

Brade waited until the door had closed behind him. Then, with his back to the bank employees, he jerked the knotted kerchief from under his collar. As he pulled it over the lower part of his face, his free hand wrapped around the butt of one of his revolvers.

At the same time, while Brade was blocking him from the sight of the bankers, Collis tugged a scarf over his own face and drew his pistol.

Brade turned. He walked toward the farmer and his wife while Collis headed for the teller. Stepping up behind the farmer, he said softly, 'Excuse me, folks."

Behind him, he heard the teller's startled gasp. He knew that in this moment, while he and Collis held the people in the bank distracted, Holgram and Goforth were covering their faces and drawing guns. They'd flank the door while he and Collis tended to business.

"Mister, I . . ." the farmer started as he turned. His mouth kept moving, but the words stopped. He stared at Brade's gun.

The woman saw it, too. Her eyes widened with fear for an instant. Then, very slowly, she smiled.

Brade gestured toward the center of the room. "If you folks will just move aside, I've got business with this feller." He turned the revolver toward the bank clerk, leveling it at the man's stomach.

Nudging his wife's arm, the farmer stepped back obediently. But she hesitated, still smiling.

"You're one of them Jameses, ain't you?" she asked, gazing into Brade's eyes. "I've been heared a lot of talk about you and your brother. Is that him?" She nodded toward Collis.

The kerchief muffled Brade's voice. "I'm Ulysses S. Grant."

With a shake of his head, the farmer said, "No, you're too tall for him."

"Then maybe I'm Jim Lane. If you'll excuse me, folks . . ."

The bookkeeper looked up from his paperwork, obviously annoyed by all the noise. Frowning, he called, "What's the matter?"

"Seems like your bank's getting robbed," Brade answered. "You might best step over here a minute."

The man rose slowly, lifting one hand. The other crept toward a drawer of the desk.

Brade jerked up the revolver. Swinging hard, he slammed the barrel into the side of the clerk's head. The man gasped, staggering back at the blow. Blood suddenly smeared the side of his face. He stumbled and fell, sprawling on the floor.

Shocked, the bookkeeper froze. His hand hovered over the drawer pull. White rimmed his eyes as he saw the revolver turned toward him.

Quietly, Brade said, "Don't do that."

The hovering hand trembled. The shivering began in his fingers and moved up his arm until his whole body shuddered. Swallowing hard, he caught hold of himself. But there wasn't much color left in his face.

"Suppose you come on over here," Brade said to him.

He glanced at the clerk lying on the floor. Wordlessly, he obeyed the soft command.

The clerk moaned and moved. He dragged himself to his hands and knees. Grabbing at a chair, he hauled himself stiffly to his feet. With one hand pressed against the gash on his face, he looked at Brade. He'd been suddenly and viciously attacked for no reason he could understand. He couldn't guess what might happen next. He was bad scared.

Slamming him that way had been an ugly thing, Brade thought. But it had been the quickest way to scare hell out of the other man without firing off a shot that would sound like an alarm.

He kicked open the gate in the low fence. Stepping through, he herded the bookkeeper and the clerk toward the cages until he could cover them and the teller as well. Then Collis came behind the counter to join him.

The door to the vault was standing closed. Gesturing with the gun, Brade ordered the men to open it.

"It's locked," the teller said. His voice came thick, as if the muscles of his throat were cramped tight. His face was slick with sweat and a sickly gray. Standing braced, sucking jagged breaths, he looked hard put. But his gaze on Brade was defiant.

Brade shook his head in denial. Mocking curiosity, he said to Collis, "Why do you reckon a bank would have the vault locked up right in the middle of the business day?"

"Maybe they weren't expecting any customers."

"They got some now. They got a fair big transaction to make. Bankers are supposed to be friendly and cooperative with us big customers, ain't they?"

"Sure," Collis grunted.

"How about one of you fellers tries being friendly and cooperative with us?" Brade turned to the bankers again. "Lest we get unhappy about doing business here and close out *your* accounts?"

The teller looked like he meant to stand firm. Brade faced the clerk instead. He raised his hand with the gun in it, as if he meant to swing it into the man's face again.

The clerk cowered. His mouth moved in an unintelligible protest.

It was the bookkeeper who spoke up, his voice strained, as if he were the one who'd been hurt. "It's not locked."

"Then open it."

Obediently, he twisted the handle and threw the bolt on the vault door. Leaning his weight against it, he swung it open. Brade held the feedsack out to him.

"Just fill this up. And make it quick."

He took it in hands that were trembling again. Silently, he began to sweep cash off the shelves into it. Shaking out another sack, Collis turned to emptying the money drawers.

"You won't succeed in this!" the teller said. "You'll never get out of Eastfork alive."

From behind the cages, the farmer called, "Yes they will! They'll skin your damned bank to the bone and leave you chasing your own fool tails!"

"That's right, feller," Holgram laughed.

Bitterness twisted the teller's face. "You're a bunch of Rebels, aren't you?"

Ignoring him, Brade snapped for the bookkeeper to hurry up. This business seemed to be dragging out forever. He was sweating under the kerchief. His back itched, and his leg ached. He wanted to get this over with and get the hell away.

A bulk of heavy money went into one sack. Collis took it. When the second sack had been filled and the shelves were empty, Brade herded the men back into the far corner. He held the gun on them while Collis tied them, hand and foot, and gagged them. With that done, they carried the sacks out of the cages.

The farmer and his wife stood waiting, both grinning. "Clean 'em out good, boys?" the woman asked.

Brade nodded. "I'm sorry, folks, but we're gonna have to tie you up, too."

"Reckon so," the man agreed. "Wouldn't look right if you didn't."

The whole thing had gone as smooth as cream. There'd be no alarm and no pursuit until one of the bank employees worked loose or a customer happened in and discovered them. The robbers would be well away from town by then, according to the plan.

Hefting one sack of plunder, Brade started for the door. He shoved the revolver back into his belt, covering the butt with the duster. Jerking down the mask to tuck it under his collar again, he grinned at Holgram and Goforth.

"Real nice work, Lieutenant," Holgram said.

Nodding agreement, he stepped through the doorway. He was on the walk, almost to the hitch rack, when he heard the shout.

"Bradenton!"

With a god-awful sinking feeling, he recognized the voice. He saw the caller. Little Spring stood on the steps of the café across the street. He had a revolver in each hand. As Brade spotted him, the right one lashed out smoke and thunder.

The sack Brade held jerked as the slug slammed into it. His own right hand was grabbing for a gun. In the instant that his fingers found the butt under the duster, time stopped.

With a strange encompassing clarity, he saw Little poised, half shadowed, holding both weapons. The right one was angled up, still spilling smoke. The kid's thumb was on the hammer, hauling back.

A couple of strides distant on the walk, two men had halted suddenly, as if they'd been jerked up on a sharp bit. They were very ordinary-looking men in business suits. One's mouth was open in amazement. The other'd already begun to turn as if to run away.

Brade's revolver cleared his belt. The muzzle rose toward Little Spring as he eared back the hammer. His forefinger tightened on the trigger. Through the sudden smoke and the scream of the gun, he saw Little flinch. Not hit though, he thought. Just damned close.

As he'd winced, Little had fired wild. He was trying to cock the pistol again as he ran down the steps. He threw himself into the dark mouth of the alley between the café and the hardware store. The shadows hid him. But Brade knew he'd stopped there to turn and take aim.

In a long striding run, Brade zagged across the street. The kid's third shot snapped past him, snarling as it hit stone and ricocheted.

"They're robbing the bank!" someone yelled. He thought it was one of those businessmen. There only seemed to be one. The other must have ducked to cover.

Glass shattered. Flame blossomed in the darkness of the alley as Little fired again. From somewhere behind him, Brade heard another gun bark. More fire answered, not just from Little Spring's weapon. He had a feeling all hell was breaking loose behind his back.

The hammer under his thumb caught at full cock. Halting his run, he raised his arm. The gun barrel leveled toward the alley. As his finger closed, he heard a hard footfall. The revolver lurched in his hand, spewing smoke. He lunged through the haze of it, knowing Little was running away down that alley.

Walls rose high and dark to either side. At the far end of the alleyway, he could see daylight—and the boy's figure silhouetted against it. Little didn't pause. He was visible for an instant, then gone from sight around the end of a building.

Brade stumbled on something in the shadows. Catching his balance, he looked at that open patch of sunlight. He'd almost missed seeing something moving in the courtyard behind the buildings. Little Spring taking cover?

He edged along the wall toward the mouth of the alley, certain Little was waiting to pick him off when he stepped into the light.

The courtyard was a small grassy square with clumps of hedge and patches of flowers. At the corner of the building, with his back pressed against the wall, Brade studied it. There was another alley opening into it across the way, but he didn't think Little would have run on through. No, the kid would wait and try again.

Little didn't understand the business of war, he thought. A man who meant to kill shouldn't holler and warn his quarry, the way the boy'd done. Someone who knew what he was about wouldn't have failed that first clean, clear shot. Little was jumpy, bad nervous about what he'd undertaken.

Hefting the money sack in his left hand, Brade swung it through the mouth of the alley.

Little's startled shot struck it, flinging it to one side. Brade saw the powdersmoke twist up from behind a hedge. Aiming carefully, he fired straight into the brush.

The kid screamed.

Flattening himself against the wall, within the shadows, Brade waited. The bitter, pungent scent of gunsmoke was sharp in his nostrils. It was an ugly smell.

"Brade?" Little Spring called. "I'm hurt, Brade!"

That was a damned lie, he thought. The kid's voice was too strong and certain. It had an almost sly sound to it. Little meant to lure him out. To hell with that.

"Bad?" he called back.

"Real bad. I think I'm dying," the boy answered. His voice didn't seem to come from exactly the same spot as before.

Brade studied the hedge. He decided that if it were him back there trying this trick, he'd have moved to the right. He'd be flattened on his belly, with the gun muzzle thrust through the low branches just so and his sights set on the mouth of the alley.

He moved cautiously, backstepped deeper into the darkness. Lifting the gun, he aligned the notch and pin on the hedge. Dammit, he didn't want a war with the kid. He didn't want any part of a thing like this.

"Little, give it up!" he called from the shadows, "Give it up, and go on back to Amy!"

"The devil take her!" the boy snapped. "I'm gonna kill you."

Directly in front of his sights, Brade saw leaves of the hedge move slightly. He tried again, "Give it up before you get hurt, Little."

"Dammit, face me!"

"Ambush was *your* idea, boy. You started this war. Now you got to either quit it or fight it out."

"I'll *kill* you," the boy repeated.

Brade sighed. Steadying the gun again, he squeezed the trigger.

The blast of Little's gun echoed his own. He thought the boy's shot went wild. Because the kid was hit, or just nervous reaction? He waited.

Bright sunlight spilled into the courtyard, making blazes of color like the patchwork of a quilt of the flower beds. Nothing moved. But from the distance beyond the alley behind him, Brade could hear spatterings of gunshots. He wondered what the hell was happening back there.

He wondered what had happened ahead of him. He waited through a long-drawn moment of silence.

"Oh Gawd!" Little gasped suddenly. He sounded more surprised than hurt. And Brade knew he'd been hit.

With the hammer eared back and his finger nestled gently against the trigger, he edged forward. His eyes were on the bit of hedge. The soft breeze had eaten away the powdersmoke from Little's gun, but the smell of it was still strong. It burned in Brade's nose.

He stepped into the light.

Something clicked.

It was a sound he knew. It was the click of a scear catching as a gun was cocked.

He jerked back. Lead slammed into the wall. Something gashed knifelike at his cheek. Striking, the slug had cracked brick and sent shards of it flying. He lifted his fingers and felt blood where a chip had ripped its sharp edge across his skin.

He saw the brush rustle. Just the one bit of hedge, as if a thin point of wind stirred it. But there was no wind, only the faint murmur of a breeze.

Feeling a weariness, a despair, he lined his sights on it. The revolver bucked heavily in his hand.

Little must have been on his knees instead of bellied down. He stood up, his arms outstretched, as if he were reaching for something just beyond his grasp. His empty hands closed, drawing back slowly. He looked like he'd caught the wind and was drawing it toward him. But there was no wind.

With a shudder, he leaned forward. He toppled onto the

hedge. It bent under him, then held. He was stretched out across it, like washed clothing laid out to dry.

Brade walked toward him.

His face was pressed into the bush. Hoarsely, he whimpered, "Help me. Jake, help me."

The gun was in Brade's right hand. He used his left to catch the boy's coat collar and haul him back off the hedge. But this was no trickery. He knew that even before he saw the bloodstains.

As he let the boy down onto the grass, Little's coat fell open. One red smear was high on the left shoulder. The other —the big one—was under the breastbone, just to one side of it. That was the one that mattered.

"Little," Brade said softly.

The kid's face was knotted tight shut. It loosened a bit, and the eyes slitted open. His lips worked, foam flecking them. "Lieutenant?"

"Yeah."

"Damn you." The curse was weak, a faint mumble.

"You should have stayed with Amy," Brade said. "Why the hell didn't you?"

"Didn't give a damn about me . . . was lying to me," Little answered, "Only you. *Always* you, damn you."

All so useless, so damned pointless, Brade thought as he sat back on his heels.

The boy sighed. It was a gurgly sound deep in his throat. His lashes fluttered, the eyes opening wider. Pleading, he said, "Help me, Lieutenant. I'm hurt."

"I can't help you now."

"I'm dead?"

"Yeah."

"Damn you!" There was more strength in the words this time. Effort wrenched at his face, twisting it as he tried to move. Painfully, he drew up an arm and got himself propped on it. His other hand groped across the grass. "My gun . . . kill you . . . dammit!"

The revolver was lying on the ground a long stride away. Brade stepped toward it. He started to scoop it up.

"Jake! You killed Jake!" Little's voice rose into something that was almost a scream. "I'll kill you, dammit!"

Maybe men destroyed themselves, or maybe something led them into it, no matter what they willed. Brade didn't know. He nudged the revolver with his boot. He shoved it toward the kid until it was against the outstretched fingers.

"There it is," he said. "Go ahead."

There was blood on Little's hand. Brade stood watching

the fingers stretch over the gun butt. The hand closed on it: Trembling, it inched the gun up off the grass.

Little squinted one eye, as if he tried to sight over the barrel as he lifted the revolver. His thumb quivered, reaching for the hammer. He dragged breath. Suddenly, he was coughing, choking.

"Hey, boy, easy," Brade said, dropping to one knee at his side.

Fighting for breath, Little steadied himself. His hand had dropped, but the revolver was still in it. He lifted it again, seeming as if he'd discovered a new reserve of strength. Pointing it at Brade's chest, he stared over it. His face wrinkled into an uncertain frown.

"Oh hell," he grunted, sounding disgusted. The muzzle of the gun tipped downward. It slid out of his fingers. His arm jerked. He collapsed, his body twisted, and lay face down in the grass.

Brade touched his shoulder.

"Somebody—somebody will do it," he whispered in a voice like the scraping together of dry branches. His back heaved and then was motionless. He seemed to shrivel inside his clothing, as if life were a substance of bulk that had flowed away, leaving just the dry husk of a body.

Rising, Brade muttered, "Yeah, somebody'll do it."

As he turned toward the alleyway again, he could hear the muffled thunder of gunshots echoing from the street beyond.

CHAPTER 12

It had to be a hell of an excitement there in front of the bank, Brade thought as he grabbed up the money sack. Either no one had noticed him running into this alley, or else they were all too busy to give chase. He headed toward the street.

The shooting didn't seem as wild as it had been a few moments before. It was more careful now, more studied. Men firing from cover at other men behind cover, he decided. He edged closer to the street end of the alleyway. With the cocked revolver in his hand, he looked out.

From where he stood within the shadows, he could only see a part of the street. The mound of a fallen horse lay not far from the bank entrance. A man sprawled motionless beside it. A man in a linen duster. Collis? Maybe Holgram or Goforth. He couldn't tell from here. *Dammit, not Collis,* he thought desperately, as if hoping would help.

To the other side, he could see the end of an upset wagon. Lead slammed into it, grooving wood and spattering splinters as he watched. One mule lay dead in the traces. There was no sign of the other.

A revolver appeared from behind the wagon. Then, just a part of a head. He couldn't tell who it was. The gun spat. It, and the head, jerked back out of sight.

More guns answered. The return fire was coming from the same side of the street the alley was on. From the hardware store, Brade judged, and from second-floor windows above the café or the drugstore, maybe both. He couldn't see the guns from the alley. The only way he'd be able to shoot back at them would be to run out into the street. He could lunge toward the wagon and hope like hell he reached cover behind it.

But how much good would it do?

The sack of plunder in his hand was important. It was what they'd all come here and risked their lives for. Men were dead for it already. What good would it do if they all died and lost it?

Scanning the street, he spotted another crumpled heap of pale linen near the corner. Another dead raider in a duster. He could see two dead—no, three. That was a hand stretched out limp from behind the wagon. And one man only returning fire from back there.

Three men dead, or else hurt bad enough to be dead, one man still fighting, and himself. That accounted for five of the eight. What about the other three? Could they have escaped? Who was it behind the wagon?

Almost in answer to his thought, a harsh voice called, "Stop shooting! I'm done! I'm out of powder!"

The firing stopped.

It was Dunkle who'd called for quarter. He flung out a revolver. It hit the bricks and skidded across the street, into the gutter.

Cautiously, he stepped from cover of the wagon. He walked into the middle of the street and turned around slowly. He made a full turn, with his fingers open, his empty hands held high.

He stopped facing the alleyway, but he was looking up into some second-floor window.

"Just hold it there, Mister," someone hollered at him.

He nodded submissively.

Brade glimpsed a man on the sidewalk in front of the

bank. For a moment, the man was hidden behind the upturned wagon. Then, he stepped out at Dunkle's back. Brade saw the shotgun in his hands and the look on his face.

The revolver Brade held jumped up. He shouted warning at Dunkle.

But the roar of the shotgun drowned his own shot and his shout. It rolled like the billowing thunder of artillery. Both barrels flared, gusting wild clouds of smoke.

The blast of buckshot lifted Dunkle off his feet. It slammed into him, tearing, flinging him toward the sidewalk. It dropped him into the gutter.

He fell almost directly in front of Brade. Arms and legs spread like wheel spokes from the thick pulp that had been a body. A shapeless pulp, a mush that spattered onto the sidewalk. Broken splinters of bone, a hash of meat and tatters of clothing, lumps and shreds in a thick sticky red sauce spilled onto the bricks.

Closing his eyes, Brade wheeled away from the sight.

He knew he'd missed the man with the shotgun. For an instant, he considered running out of the alley, shoving his gun into the man's gut, and triggering it.

He'd be trading off his own life doing that. And it wouldn't buy anything but a moment of satisfaction. Right now, he was holding half the plunder that the raiders had come here for. His business was to get the hell away from this town with it and see that it was passed along to Logan's friend in St. Louis—if he could.

As he turned toward the courtyard again, he heard voices. There were people back there now, too. They'd find Little Spring's body. They'd be coming through the alley in a minute. He was pinned here—trapped between the ones in the yard and the crowd that had begun to fill the street.

The breath choked in his throat, cramped as if a noose had been snugged around his neck. Glancing toward the street, he caught at and balanced the tensions in him. With a taut, desperate calm, he told himself there was only one way out. Straight ahead.

People milled around the dead men, babbling to each other with frenzy-edged enthusiasm. They giggled and gazed intently at the remains of havoc.

Brade peeled and dropped the duster. He flung down the slouch hat and buttoned his suit coat over the revolvers in his belt. Holding the sack of loot at his side, against his leg, he stepped out of the alley.

Running footsteps clattered in the alley behind him. A couple of half-grown boys dashed through into the street.

"There's a dead man back there in the yard!" one shouted.

"One here, too," the other said in sudden awe, staring at what had been Dunkle.

The first one turned toward Brade. "What happened, Mister?"

"Somebody tried to rob the bank."

"They sure got blasted," the kid grinned.

Brade nodded.

"Were you in the fighting? You got blood on your face."

He touched his fingers to the cut on his cheek. The blood felt dry. He rubbed at it, afraid it wouldn't wipe off. Bad afraid it would attract attention to him.

The kids shoved into the mob. Brade looked past them toward the bank. Between the heads of bystanders, he could glimpse the hitch rack. His bay was gone, but Collis' speedy little mare was still at the rail. Working along the edge of the crowd, behind their backs, he started toward her.

As he came up beside her, he eyed the saddle pockets. The whole sack of loot would never fit into one of them. And he damned well couldn't start divvying the greenbacks between both pockets here and how. He'd have to chance carrying the sack right out in the open.

"Mister James?"

It was a woman's voice in a hushed half-whisper. He thought he recognized it.

With the taut calmness in him fine-drawn, he turned to face the farm woman who'd been in the bank. In the flash of panic that lashed through him, he wondered if he could fling himself onto the mare and somehow manage to outrun the bullets that would follow him.

She smiled. "Down the coach road to the south, about six miles, there's wagon ruts that turn off to the left. Right by a dead elm trunk. Couple miles along it, you'll come to our place. Ain't much. Plank house painted red. If you happen past that way, we'd be pleased of your company."

"I'd be right happy to get there," he said hoarsely.

"You got blood on your face."

He rubbed at it with the back of his wrist.

Glancing at the sack that hung from his other hand, she held up her market basket. There was a checkered cloth over it. As she lifted the cloth, she told him, "You shouldn't carry that around here. I'll tote it home if you want. It'll be waiting there for you."

He had a feeling she really meant it. Stuffing the sack into the basket, he muttered, "I'm obliged to you."

She nodded in acknowledgment. Still smiling, she turned away from him and pushed into the crowd.

His hands trembled as he unlooped the mare's reins. He

led her, walking along the edge of the crowd, looking over shoulders. But he couldn't see who the dead men were from there. And he didn't dare try for a closer look.

He glimpsed a face in the mob across the way. And suddenly, there was ice in his blood. Sharp needles of it speared through his whole body, almost tearing apart the calmness he clung to.

It was a face he'd seen before. Too often before. For the first time, he realized he'd seen it in that cold frozen instant when Little Spring had stood across the street shooting at him. Then, he'd barely noticed the two very ordinary men on the walk. He hadn't paid enough attention to recognize that bland, sandy-moustached face with its pale blue eyes then.

Now, he saw it again, and he knew the man. Orin Coleman.

For an instant, their eyes met. Coleman blinked. He was looking past Brade, gazing into the distance at nothing in particular in a dull, disinterested way.

Brade didn't believe it. He had a god-awful feeling that Coleman recognized him—each time. He felt certain Coleman knew him for one of the robbers. But if that was so, why the devil didn't the man do something about it?

It took effort to keep walking calmly, leading the mare around the crowd. Fighting the ache in his leg, he managed to keep his stride even. At the corner, he rose to the saddle and lifted reins. Struggling against the urge to look back—against the urge to slam his spurs into her sides and run like hell—he ambled her toward the bridge.

He was across it when he heard the clatter of hooves on the cobbles behind him. Glancing over his shoulder, he recognized them for a posse. A dozen or more men on horseback, some with guns over their saddle bows, galloped toward him. *At* him?

He knew he couldn't escape by running. Either they had him—or they were heading out to hunt the few robbers who'd escaped. And maybe he could bluff his way out.

Reining the mare to the side of the street, he held her there and watched the posse rumble toward him. An innocent man would be curious, he thought. He gazed at them, hoping his face was curious.

The leaders went past him. But one man jerked rein, wheeling toward him. He stared at Orin Coleman.

"Posse," Coleman called breathlessly. "Chasing bank robbers! Come on along!"

Another man stopped at Coleman's side and added, "We need every man we can get, Mister. You got any firearms?"

"Pistol," Brade muttered.

"Come on along!" the man said eagerly.

Touching spurs to the mare's flanks, Brade fell in with the posse. Coleman maneuvered to his side.

Half grinning, looking like a stranger just trying to strike up a friendly conversation, he said, "We'll catch them. Eventually, we'll get them *all*."

Brade wasn't sure whether he'd heard a significant emphasis or not. Coleman managed to seem innocent of any subtle intent. He looked as harmless as he sounded.

Making no answer, Brade studied him from the corner of his eye. The man acted too damned innocent. He just aggravated that icy wariness lying along Brade's spine.

After a moment, Brade asked, "Just who are we chasing?"

"Bank robbers," Coleman said. "Three of 'em got onto their horses and got away. Probably the same men who robbed the bank in Serena."

The man on the other side of Brade spoke up. "They all run off in this direction. Ain't many places for 'em to hole up around here. At least one of 'em was hit, hurt bad. They won't get far." He laughed and added, "Just to the ends of a couple of strong ropes."

"I don't hold lynching," Coleman said. He seemed to look past Brade at the man. But Brade had the feeling those pale eyes were intent on him all the while.

Ahead, one of the leaders shouted and waved to stop them. They pulled rein, clustering around him.

"Road forks yonder. Half you fellers stay with me. Other half follow Steve here over toward the old mill ruins." He brought down his hand as if he was slicing the posse in two with a long knife.

As Brade fell in with the bunch that would be heading toward the mill, he was aware of Coleman reining sharply to stay at his flank. He glanced over his shoulder.

Coleman blinked, and his eyes were as blank as ever. Too damned blank. They were a mask, hiding something. But what? If Coleman did recognize him and know him for a raider, why the hell didn't the man speak up?

Dull gray clouds spread across the day, threatening to spill rain. The smell of it was in the air. Not a storm, Brade thought, but a drizzle. The kind that would hang on, soaking through a man's clothes and his skin if he didn't find shelter.

A few of the posse men muttered to each other about it. They'd been riding for several hours now and were wearying of the fruitless chase. They began to suggest getting back home before the rain began.

The one called Steve, their leader, cursed and answered that they had work to do. With an ugly enthusiasm, he reminded them that they had to catch and lynch some robbers.

One man swallowed his pride and quit, but the rest hung on, following Steve along the trace that wound through the woods lining the creek. It was damp under the trees and twilight dark. Scanning the shadows, Brade told himself a halfway skilled bushwacker could hide easily in there. The men who'd ridden into Eastfork were all skilled. He figured they were safe enough from this clumsy posse.

He glanced sideways at Coleman. The man clung at his side as if they were chained together. Why?

Something moved in the woods. As Brade glimpsed it, one of the posse men gave a shout. Wheeling off the trace, Steve plunged toward the shadow, hollering for the posse to follow.

It looked like a man on horseback. Brade stared at it, thinking none of the bushwackers would be fool enough to show himself that way.

The horseman suddenly flung a shot toward them.

A damn fool, Brade thought as the riders around him burst into wild shouting and began to fire back. They spattered lead into the shadows and the trees. Powdersmoke caught under the branches, adding its haze to the half-darkness.

Brade drew his pistol. He didn't intend to shoot at the fleeing shadow. And he didn't want to waste the lead. Hoping that in the confusion no one would notice he wasn't firing, he squinted over the sights. He couldn't make out the horseman as more than a dark figure.

The horse was running raggedly through the brush. It angled away, then swung around, heading almost directly toward the posse. Brade saw then that the man on its back was leaning far out of the saddle. The horse swerved again. The man fell.

Spreading out, the posse men surrounded him. From the way he was lying motionless, face down in the weeds, he looked dead. With a silent curse, Brade halted the mare and hurried to join the other men who'd dismounted.

They made a circle around the fallen man and stood staring at him uncertainly. Brade shoved past them, dropping to one knee. As he touched the man's shoulder, he was aware of another person kneeling at his side. He knew without a glance that it was Orin Coleman.

But at this moment, he had no concern for Coleman. The downed rider was Bob Alan Logan. Gently, Brade turned him onto his back. The flesh of Logan's face was warm to his fingers. He felt a faint motion.

Swallowing back the sour taste in his mouth, clinging to a

calmness worn almost to snapping, Brade said, "He's alive."

The only response was from one of the posse men at his back. With a happy sound, the man said, "I got a rope."

Brade clamped his mouth shut on a curse. He was tempted to take a look at the one who'd spoken. He wanted to know which face it was, in case he ever saw it over his gunsights. But saving a life mattered a damn sight more than avenging a death. Maybe, with luck, Logan wouldn't die. Logan *couldn't* die. He was the one who knew the man in St. Louis. He was the one who could salvage the remnants of this damned fiasco of a raid.

With hands that felt awkward and close to shaking, Brade fumbled open the front of Logan's shirt. He found a broad patch of blood smearing the shirt on the right side, just above the waist. As he tugged out the shirttail, Logan moaned softly.

"What you doing?" someone asked, sounding curious and stupid.

"He's bad hurt, but he's still alive," Brade grunted. He pulled the sheath knife from under his coat and slit Logan's undersuit. The blood was caked. The wound was at least several hours old. Carefully, Brade peeled the flannel back from it.

"We can't hang around here playing doctor to no bank robber," Steve protested. "We got two more of these sons to catch."

Brade didn't dare look up at him. The man might read too much in his face. He muttered, "Go ahead. Go catch them. I'll tend this one and get him back to town."

Quickly—too quickly—Coleman volunteered, "I'll help."

The chill lay along Brade's spine. He glanced at Coleman, hating and fearing what he couldn't understand. But Logan was more important at this moment. He turned his attention back to the wound.

The ball seemed to have gone in at a sharp angle. It might not have hit anything vital, Brade thought hopefully. Could be just pain and spilled blood that had Logan unconscious.

He heard Steve muttering uncertainly. Why didn't that bastard go on with his hot-blooded manhunt?

Coleman pointed to Logan's torn and dark-stained sleeve. "His arm's busted up, too. He needs a surgeon."

"He needs a gravedigger," Steve said. "Leave him lie. We can collect the carcass later."

Brade didn't answer. As he pressed his kerchief against the trickle of blood that had started fresh from the bullet hole, he knew Coleman was studying him intently.

"Hell," Steve grunted. "Come on, men. We got work. You two are just wasting your time here."

"It's *our* time," Brade said. He heard the posse men begin to move. Leather creaked as they mounted up. He looked to Coleman. "Hold this here, will you?"

Coleman's hand slid over his, keeping the kerchief firm in place. He moved around Logan then, using the knife to cut open the bloody sleeve. The posse men sat watching him a moment longer, then began riding away.

The injury to Logan's arm looked bad. The ball had gone into the back of the elbow, shattering bone. A surgeon would probably take the arm off, he thought. He asked Coleman, "You got anything I can use for bandaging?"

Coleman handed him a large white linen pocket kerchief, then began tearing strips off Logan's shirttail. As he did it, he asked conversationally, "You've had experience with wounds before?"

"In the war," Brade muttered. Taking the strips Coleman held out, he started to wrap the damaged elbow as firmly as he could. Logan winced, groaning.

Brade's hands were busy, his eyes intent on what he was doing. He concentrated, trying to be as gentle as he could. As he tied the last knot, he said, "Step over to the crick and fetch a wet cloth, would you?"

"Maybe *you'd* better do that," Coleman said coldly.

Startled, Brade looked toward him. There was a revolver in his hand. It was a four-barreled pocket pistol that looked a little like an undersized pepper box. It was aimed straight at Brade's chest.

"First, you'd best ease the pistols out of your belt and put them down on the ground," Coleman told him. "And, please, don't make me use this."

Brade pulled back his coat and caught one gun butt between his thumb and forefinger. He dragged the gun out of his belt and set it in the grass. Slowly and deliberately, he set the second one next to it. The four-muzzled pistol aimed at him was small, but close enough to be thoroughly deadly. Four aces, and Coleman seemed too cool to fluster and make a mistake with a hand like that.

"You want water for him, go ahead and get it," Coleman said then. "I'll be right behind you."

"I need a kerchief, cloth of some kind," Brade muttered.

"Tear a piece off that feed sack you were carrying in Eastfork."

"I ain't got it with me."

"The hell! Who has it?"

It was the first time Brade had seen any real animation in

Coleman's face. Angry disappointment flashed in the pale blue eyes. Coleman glared at him.

"That what you want?" Brade asked. "The money?"

"Yeah."

"I could take you to it. I'd buy that pistol off you. Pay you a damned high price for it." He gestured slightly at the gun Coleman leveled toward him.

"Right now, you don't have enough money to buy this pistol."

"I might know where there's plenty of it. A sack full of greenbacks. Plenty of money."

"Not enough," Coleman answered. "I'd want more. I'd want a share in the next raid you plan."

So that was it. Coleman wanted to join the robbers. For a moment, it all made sense. But then it fell apart.

Brade stared at him, thinking nobody in his right mind would be asking into a gang that had just been shot to hell and gone and had posses sieving the woods for what was left of it.

Maybe Coleman wasn't in his right mind. But he seemed too steady, too sure of himself, to be telling the truth.

Forcing a grin, Brade said, "If that's what you want, you got it."

There was a flicker of satisfaction in Coleman's face. But the pistol in his hand didn't move at all. With his eyes on it, Brade tried reaching a hand cautiously toward his own guns.

"Just wait a minute," Coleman snapped.

Brade eased back, knowing nothing had really changed. He watched Coleman scoop up a revolver and stuff it into his belt.

Picking up the second one, smiling slightly, Coleman said, "It'll be best if I carry the firearms for the time being."

"Do it your way," Brade shrugged. "I don't give a damn. But my friend here is bad hurt. I got to get him to help."

"In town?"

He shook his head. "I got a place to take him."

The look of satisfaction flashed in Coleman's face again. He nodded agreement.

"Got to get him onto a horse," Brade said, glancing around. His mount and Coleman's were still there, but the horse Logan had been riding before was gone.

"Use your horse. You can ride double and hold him," Coleman said. It wasn't a suggestion, but an order.

Logan couldn't be draped over the saddle with that bullet hole in him. He'd have to be set astride. Coleman held the mare's reins in one hand, keeping the pistol in the other, while Brade dragged Logan onto his feet.

He made a move at hefting the limp body up. It didn't seem to work. Catching his breath, holding Logan propped against him, he said, "Look, Coleman, I can't do this alone. You shin up behind the saddle and haul while I lift."

Coleman hesitated warily. He looked at the injured man in Brade's arms. Then, pocketing the pistol, he swung up onto the mare's rump. He took hold of Logan with both hands, pulling as Brade shoved.

Finally, the injured man was in the saddle. Coleman held him there as Brade tied his ankles to the girth. He'd secured the right leg and was starting to the nigh side of the horse to tie the other one when he saw Logan's good hand move slightly, fingers wrapping into the mare's mane. He glanced at Logan's face.

The lashes fluttered. Logan was watching him from under them. He gave a slight nod and stepped on around the horse.

It wasn't Logan's ankle he reached for. Grabbing Coleman by the leg, he jerked hard.

Startled, off balance, Coleman tumbled backward. The mare shied, swinging her rump. With a crowhop, she shot out her hind hooves.

As he flung himself toward the falling man, Brade heard the thud. He saw Coleman sprawl, with blood slicking a streak across the side of his head. The mare's iron shoe had caught him.

Kneeling, Brade took the pistol out of Coleman's pocket and retrieved his own revolvers. Then, he put a hand to Coleman's face. He tested the wound with his fingertips. It seemed as if the mare's hoof had just glanced, peeling a swath of skin. Didn't feel like there was any broken bone under it.

"Dead?" Logan's voice grated like a mill wheel just beginning to move.

"No." Brade clambered to his feet and took up the mare's reins. She'd bolted a long stride, then stopped and look back. She stood peaceably to be caught. He looked up at Logan's pale, grim face. "How are you?"

"Not dead. Feel close to it, though. Hurt like hell."

"You'll be all right. We got friends not far from here."

"Huh?"

"Yeah. Don't worry. We'll get there."

"That one," Logan glanced toward Coleman. "Who?"

"Damned if I know. Some kind of slick liar. Pinkerton, maybe."

"Kill him."

Brade looked at the unconscious man and shook his head.

"Kill him," Logan repeated.

"No, dammit! Maybe he ain't a Pinkerton. Maybe he's just some kind of poor damned fool like the rest of us." Brade turned away, heading for Coleman's horse.

"Lieutenant!" Logan growled at his back. "An order . . ."

He stepped up to the saddle and wheeled the horse over to Logan's side. As he reached out to catch up the mare's reins, he answered, "To hell with orders. To hell with this whole damned war!"

Gigging his mount into a trot, he led the mare behind him. Logan, helpless in the saddle, made no more protest. But Brade could sense his anger. And he understood it.

He had a feeling he was making a bad mistake leaving Coleman alive.

CHAPTER 13

Logan slumped unconscious in the saddle. Keeping the pace easy, Brade hunted out the coach road, then skirted along it, staying to the wood. The rain had begun, a thin drizzle that wasn't cold but damnably wet. It soaked into his hair and trickled down his face. Ducking his head against it, he wiped at his eyes and searched for wheel ruts turning left past a dead elm.

The sounds of riders on the road ahead sent him to cover in the brush. Through the branches, he watched the horsemen coming uproad, heading toward the town. They were posse men, but they seemed to have forgotten their chase. With their hats pulled low and their faces turned down, they looked concerned with nothing more than getting to shelter.

Once they were well past, Brade moved onto the road. Finding the wagon tracks at last, he followed them to a red plank house. His hallo brought the farmer to the door, carrying a shotgun.

The farmer recognized him and motioned him back toward the barn, then dashed through the rain to join him. Together, they carried Logan into the house. He was still unconscious when they bedded him on a pallet that the farmer's wife laid out on the kitchen floor. As soon as that was done, the woman hurried to fetch the sack of loot to Brade.

Peeling his damp coat, he crouched by the hearth fire and dumped the bank plunder on the floor. Most of the hard money had been in the sack Collins had carried. There was only a handful of coin in this one. The rest was paper, mostly greenbacks. He picked up a couple and held them toward the farmer.

As the man reached for them, his wife spoke up. "We can't take that. Not rightly."

"The hell you can't. It's the least you can take."

Drawing back his hand, the farmer shook his head.

"Take it," Brade insisted.

The woman had set in to simmering isinglass for court plaster to bandage Logan's wounds. She peered intently into the kettle as she muttered, "No, we just can't."

There was something wrong, Brade thought. Watching her warily, he asked, "Why not?"

"Wouldn't be right." She still didn't look toward him.

He figured she wasn't willing to meet his eyes. What was she trying to hide? He said, "On account of you mean to sell us out?"

She jerked her head up. Her cheeks reddened as she faced him. "No sir! No, we—I—truth is, Mister, we already tooken ten dollars out of that poke. We—I know it was wrong, but there was so much, didn't seem like you'd miss it none. We didn't rightly mean to *steal* from you, Mister."

Brade laughed. The fine-drawn tension snapped. He doubled over in wild laughing. It was only partly in amazement at her confession. Mostly, it was pure relief.

She stared at him with a puzzled, concerned frown. "Mister James, you all right?"

He caught at his breath. His ribs were beginning to ache. Waving the bills toward her, he said, "Take it. We won't miss it."

She accepted the money hesitantly. "We're obliged to you. You don't hardly know how obliged."

Logan groaned. As if the scent of greenbacks had wakened him, he blinked open his eyes and mumbled, "What's the matter?"

"Nothing," Brade answered, still grinning and gulping breath. But as he looked at the stacks of bills he'd sorted out on the floor, the feeling of amusement faded. The job was damn far from done yet. "Logan, we got about three thousand in paper money here, and some bonds and things like that. I figure I ought to get it to this friend of yours in St. Louis."

Logan grunted. Brade wasn't sure whether or not it was meant as agreement.

"What's his name? How do I find him?"

"No."

"What do you mean *no?*"

"Not you—*me.*"

"Huh?"

"To St. Louis," Logan muttered. He sounded as if he were slipping back into unconsciousness. "You get me to St. Louis, then him."

"The hell! You're too bad busted up to travel."

"Surgeons in St. Louis—get me there." He sighed, sucked his breath and scowled, struggling to keep talking. "Get me there, Lieutenant. *He*'ll take care of me—see I get the best. What I know, he'll *have* to take care of me—to him, Lieutenant."

"I *can't* take you," Brade protested.

The farmer cleared his throat. Looking as if it hurt him to say it, he put in, "You can't just leave him here, Mister. We can bed you and help you tonight, but we can't noways keep him till he's healed. There's posses hunting you now. I seen 'em already. They'll keep hunting. They don't find you, they'll take a notion you're hid out with somebody. They'll want to look through the house and into the barn. If they was to find you or him here, they'd burn us out!"

"That's the truth of it," his wife added.

Brade swallowed back the surge of anger. The farmer was right. He and his wife had already accepted a fair piece of danger to themselves in helping this much. He couldn't ask them to take on more of *his* troubles. Squatting on his haunches, he gazed at the money as he studied the problem. He was aware of the man and woman watching him, waiting for his answer.

After a long moment, he asked, "Does the railroad from Eastfork run straight through to St. Louis?"

The farmer nodded.

"They'd sure notice at the depot if I tried taking him onto the cars, the shape he's in," Brade said thoughtfully. "Unless maybe I could get him onto a freight car without anybody saw us."

"Ma's got a cousin works in the yards," the man told him. "He might could help you."

"You think he'd be willing?" he looked from the farmer to the woman. "And be quiet about it afterwards? There'd be a few greenbacks in it for him."

A smile of relief spread across her face. "He'd be glad of the chance. He's a good Southerner. He'd be real glad to help you fellers."

Brade grinned back at her, then looked at Logan again. He wondered whether it could work. Logan seemed really bad hurt.

But a night's sleep helped the injured man a lot. He woke to complain that he was hungry. The woman dosed him with laudanum, bound his wounds with court plaster, and set out a hearty breakfast for him and Brade. He managed to walk to the table. As he settled into a chair, he grinned at Brade.

Waiting while the woman finished her cooking, Brade had been cleaning and reloading his pistols. They lay beside his plate.

Eyeing them, Logan said, "I need a gun."

Brade gave a shake of his head. "You couldn't handle one."

"The hell I couldn't! I need a gun, Lieutenant. We might run into trouble. I *need* one."

He studied on Logan as he thought about it. The man didn't look strong enough to use one of the heavy revolvers, even with only a half charge of powder for each load. And he damned sure didn't want to give up one of his own handguns anyway.

Reaching into his coat pocket, he brought out the little pistol he'd taken off Coleman. It was small and light. And not likely to be of much use to him. Once the four shots in it were used up, he hadn't any more of those thirty-two caliber rimfire cartridges for it.

He shoved it toward Logan. "Take this. Don't try using it unless things get really bad though."

"What the hell kind of toy is this?" Logan picked it up and scowled at it.

"Ain't exactly a toy. It's a Remington-Elliot, and the way I've heard, it'll do the job if you're close up enough on whatever you're shooting at."

"Loaded?"

"All four barrels."

Logan settled it into his palm, sliding a finger through the trigger ring.

"Mind out," Brade said. "It's self-acting. You push that ring forward, you got it cocked. Back again, and it fires. Handle it careful."

"Well, I suppose any firearm's better than none," Logan grumbled, dropping it into his pocket.

Poorly as he looked, he was damned determined, Brade thought, watching him set into the food the woman put in front of him. Maybe he had determination enough to get him through the ordeal of the trip. With luck, they might make it to St. Louis all right. It was sure as hell time for luck to start running with them again.

Brade felt better himself when he'd finished eating. The ache in his head had about faded away. There was some stiffness in his bones, but nothing bad. The scarred thigh bothered him some as he stood up and stretched. He ignored it.

While her husband harnessed the team, the woman bundled some food for them to take along. She tucked what was left of the laudanum into the croker sack with the food and the bank loot.

Brade helped Logan into the wagon. The farmer spread a tarpaulin over them, then started the horses. Leaning into the traces, they jolted the wagon into motion.

They were stopped once on the road. Holding his breath, clutching a revolver, Brade listened to the voices of the posse men. A young bunch, he thought. And as eager as if they were on a wolf hunt. He sighed with relief when the wagon lurched and began to roll again.

The next stop was at the railroad yards. Like the woman had said, her cousin was glad to help. Especially when he saw the handful of greenbacks Brade was willing to pay.

It was sticky, stifling hot inside the car. And the trip in the wagon hadn't gone easy with Logan. Brade got him settled, gave him more of the laudanum, and then sat down by the door, hoping to catch a little air through the narrow crack that had been left open.

The cars made good time, but they jolted something awful. Logan slept fitfully, thrashing his good hand and muttering about fires. Brade wondered whether he was dreaming about the past or about hell to come.

There was rain that afternoon. It didn't cool things off any, but only made the thick hot air inside the car stickier. By sunset, the drizzle tapered off into a windy dampness. Miasmas rose from the swamps outlying St. Louis. Long shadows merged into heavy haze. Brade felt weary, in bad need of more sleep himself, when he shook Logan awake.

The cars were beginning to slow for the switch that the yardman had warned him about. He watched through the crack in the door, trying to judge the timing. They'd have to wait until they were out of sight of the switchman, but they couldn't wait too long, or the train would pick up speed again.

He saw the man with the lantern at trackside. Passing him, the train swung into a long curve. As Brade heaved open the door, he thought this was going to be damned hard on Logan. It *could* kill him. But there wasn't any other way.

Logan poised, crouching with his good arm wrapped over the one in the sling. His face was a putty gray in the dim light. His eyelids looked thick, the eyes under them unseeing. He mumbled something hoarsely. Brade couldn't make out the words. But there wasn't time to worry about it.

"Now!" he hollered.

Logan flung himself through the door. Brade saw him tumble to his knees, drop, and roll. Over the screeching whine of the iron wheels, he thought he heard a scream of pain. The locomotive's whistle wailed, as if in mockery of it.

There was a sick hollowness in Brade's gut as he threw himself through the door. He hit ground rolling, sliding with loose rock ballast. Coming up onto his knees, he spotted Logan's limp form back a ways alongside the roadbed.

Sickly afraid of what he'd find, he got to his feet and hurried toward the injured man.

Logan was still alive. But he was unconscious and groaning softly as he drew shallow breaths. Brade wet his kerchief in a puddle and wiped at the pain-taut face. It didn't seem to help.

The long shadows were fading rapidly into night. Ahead, he could see the lanterns in the St. Louis yards. Beyond them were the glows and specks of city lights. He hunkered at Logan's side, glad for the dusk that provided cover of a sort. At least he didn't have to get Logan moved to shelter immediately.

Far off, a river steamer gave a moan of its whistle, calling hands on the levee to be ready to receive it. The sound was mournful lonely. A lost and pleading sound that woke echoes of itself in Brade. This was a hell of a place to be, and a hell of a spot to be in, he thought. But he and Logan had made it this far. They were past the worst of it. All that was left now was to get Logan and the plunder safely to the mysterious friend. Then, he could rest.

He wet the kerchief again and wiped at Logan's face with it. Mumbling hoarse curses, Logan woke. He flailed his arm, trying to prop himself up on it.

"Hold still. Rest yourself a minute more," Brade said.

He didn't seem to understand. He kept muttering about getting the fires to burning and getting away.

"That'll bring him around," he gasped thinly, "Damn fine trick. Never know it was us. Jayhawkers. Always blame jayhawkers."

"Easy," Brade whispered, wiping at his face again. Dreaming about the war, he figured. He'd had dreams like that too damned often himself. Dreams filled with the stench of Lawrence burning.

Logan calmed. His lips kept moving, muttering more faint curses. Suddenly he said, "Bradenton!"

"Yes, sir?"

He'd sounded surprised. After a moment, he said it again, more naturally.

"You awake now?" Brade asked him.

He grunted.

"Think you can move?"

"Yeah. You got to help me, Lieutenant."

Brade took hold of his good arm, stretching it over his shoulder. Bearing Logan's weight against his side, he rose cautiously to his feet. Logan leaned heavily against him, gasping breath. He stood holding the man until the breathing steadied. Then, he took a step. Logan moved with him.

The ground away from the road bed had looked like a grassy plain. But under the grass, it was a thick, slippery mud that clutched at their boots, squishing and sucking. It was a damned lot of work for Brade to haul Logan across it and locate the coach road. By the time he'd found it, the night was full dark and thick with mosquitoes.

He lowered Logan to the berm of the road and sat down to rest himself. Around them, frogs had taken up a noisy gabbling. Bugs swarmed over them, buzzing and stinging. He brushed futilely at them, his eyes closed against the ones that wanted to walk on his eyeballs. It was a poor rest that they were letting him take.

"Where from here?" he asked Logan.

"We on the coach road?"

"Yeah."

"Toward town. Houses on low bluff, near the river. Not far. Fork left."

"You think we're gonna be able to find it in the dark?"

"Yeah. Easy. Not far."

"All right," he sighed. "Let's get moving. Get away from this damned swamp."

Logan leaned more and more heavily on him as they walked on. The stars and broken moon curtained by a damp haze didn't give much light for a man hunting his way in strange country. He almost missed the fork. Once he was on it, he stopped to rest again.

They were on higher ground here. The bugs weren't quite so bad. He rubbed at his tired eyes and blinked at the blurs of lamplight marking clusters of houses off to either side of the road. Concentrating, he could hear faint sounds like water. The river lapping at its banks, he hoped. It couldn't be much farther. It damned well better not be. He was exhausted, and Logan seemed barely conscious now.

Gazing into the misty darkness, he thought of fields springing green with young corn and flax and a house with smoke curling up from the chimney. A cookfire on the hearth giving up scents of food-making. A girl tending the cooking.

He shook his head against the near-dream he'd drifted into. Couldn't let himself fall asleep now. Time for dreaming later, once this damned job was done. Struggling, he got Logan onto his feet and moving again.

There had been dirt under his feet. Suddenly, he came onto cobbles, then onto a winding street dotted with puddles of light from pole lamps. Dark fronts of houses lined it. The sight of them stirred Logan into a determined awareness. He pointed out the house, and Brade headed for it.

Lanterns like carriage lamps flanked the door. They were lit, showing it to be a big box of a house, built city style, with stairs up to a high stoop. There was an iron fence backed with hedge and a small strip of lawn between the street and the house. A driveway led past one side, probably to a stable in the back. The gates were open.

Brade went through them, cutting across the grass to the steps. Logan was managing to walk, but his weight seemed to be all on Brade's side. Clinging to the railing with one hand, he dragged Logan up the stairs.

A polished brass knocker glinted on the door. He lifted it and slammed it down hard. He could hear the echo inside.

"Only one servant," Logan mumbled. "Drives for him, too. Maybe out."

"Hell," Brade grunted. He cupped his hand against the panel of glass beside the door and tried to look through. It was too dark inside for him to see anything.

"You're *sure* this is the right place?" he asked.

"Yeah. Sure."

"All right, I'll get us inside."

"Upstairs. Sort of office. Get me there."

Sighing, Brade took Logan's weight again. From the driveway, he could make out the form of the carriage house. It was dark. He hauled Logan to the back steps and left him clinging to the railing.

The back door was latched, but there were glass panes in it. He broke out one with the butt of a revolver and reached through to pull the latch. Then, he went back for Logan.

Inside the kitchen, he lit a match to orient himself.

"Hallway," Logan muttered, pointing toward a closed door. "Stairs. Upstairs."

The staircase was steep. By the time they reached the top, Logan was about out of strength. And Brade didn't feel far from it. Pausing, he leaned against the wall and sucked breath as he lit another match. It flared, stinking of sulphur and showing him another hallway similar to the one downstairs. Logan gestured at a door toward the front of the building.

This one wasn't locked. Brade kicked it open. Big windows

to the street let in traces of moonlight. He could make out the dark shapes of furniture.

"Sofa," Logan grunted.

Brade spotted it and maneuvered Logan across the room to ease him down onto it.

Striking another match, Brade asked, "You think I'd better have a look at those wounds?"

"No! No light!"

"All right." He scanned the room quickly before he shook out the flame. There was a sideboard by the door, with a full decanter and some glasses on it. Groping in the dim light, he poured for himself and Logan.

At first, he had to hold Logan's head up and put the glass to the man's lips. But the liquor seemed to fire Logan's strength and determination. After a few moments, he insisted on sitting propped up against the corner of the sofa. Despite the shakiness of his hand, he wanted to hold the glass for himself.

Brade felt too tired to argue it. He let Logan have his own way. With a glass in one hand and the decanter in the other, he settled himself in the swivel chair behind the desk against the far wall. Wearily, he put his feet up on the desk, leaned back, and let his eyes close.

Logan's voice called him from half-drowsing. "Well, we made it, Brade. We got here."

Brade drew a deep sighing breath and took another sip of the brandy. He wondered if he'd been asleep long. Logan sounded a lot stronger, more rested. Maybe strong enough to answer a few questions.

"How'd it happen back there in Eastfork?"

"Damn-fool kid begun to shoot at you, set loose hell," Logan told him. "One of the men across the street give a holler and hightailed into the hardware store. Come out with a repeating rifle . . ."

"The one with the sandy moustache and blue eyes?"

"Hell, I didn't notice. What I seen was he begun shooting at us. Others then. Come running from everywheres. Handguns, rifles, shotguns. Everywhere. People in the buildings sticking guns out the windows. They had us in crossfire." He paused, catching breath. Or remembering. "Cutting us down like hell. Hit me 'fore I could get onto my horse. I made it, though."

"You'll be all right," Brade muttered.

"I *always* make it. My friend, he'll take care of me. He's *got* to." Logan's voice was growing vague again. "All I done for him, he'll look out for me."

Even in the thin moonlight, Brade could see that the walls

of the room were lined with shelves of books. He'd felt the softness of the carpet underfoot. The sofa he'd stretched Logan out on had seemed like a fine piece of furniture. A real fancy house, he thought.

"He's a moneyed gentleman from the look of this place."

"Plenty of money," Logan mumbled. "Me, too."

Brade frowned into the darkness. "Your friend seems to have come through the war right well for a Secesh sympathizer."

"Smart man. Smart like me. Takes a smart man to make a profit on a war. An' a profit on the peace."

He didn't like the sound of it at all. This house, Logan's rambling words, the whole business had a wrongness about it. Feeling the ice of apprehension along his spine, Brade straightened in the chair. He leaned forward as he asked, "*Who* is this friend of yours?"

If Logan heard, he either didn't understand, or else he just ignored the question. Sounding as sad as if something had come to an end, he murmured, "You been a good soldier, Lieutenant. Too good a soldier. You'd have made a better man for me if you wasn't. Only you can't change your ways of thinking, can you?"

"What do you mean by that?" He started to his feet. Carrying the decanter, he dropped to one knee at Logan's side.

Logan seemed almost unconscious again, but a little of the liquor brought him around.

"What are you talking about?" Brade demanded of him. "Who the devil is this friend of yours?"

"Friend, Lieutenant. Good friend. You hear something?"

Brade nodded, rising. Hooves clattered on cobbles and wheels rattled. He turned toward the windows.

In the street below, he could see the carriage drawing up. It stopped at the gate, and a man stepped out. The figure was lean and lanky, vaguely familiar. Frowning, trying to place it, he watched the carriage pull away toward the drive. The man came through the gate and up the walk to the front door.

A sharp click broke the silence.

Brade knew the sound and knew it was close behind his back. He started to wheel away from the window that silhouetted him to Logan.

Thunder exploded in the room, slamming into him. A whiplash jar shocked his whole body, catching him like a charging bull, flinging him against the wall.

There was no pain, no feeling at all. It was as if the jolt had broken his mind free of his body. He knew what had happened and what was happening. He saw Logan dimly in the moonlight, his good hand outstretched with the little four-shooter in it.

There was another click as Logan cocked it again.

Without feeling it, Brade knew that his own hand had jerked a revolver from his belt as he'd turned. The hand lifted the gun, and he saw the hammer and muzzle align in front of his eye. Beyond them, he saw Logan.

Light burst in a brilliant flare that filled his eyes. Through the roar of Logan's second shot, Brade heard glass shatter. Shards of the broken window showered behind him.

The glare of Logan's shot was still in his eyes as his own gun jumped. It threw itself out of his fingers.

His ears rang with the echo of the blasts inside the closed room. The gunfire was an afterimage blurring his vision. He smelled the thick stink of the smoke. But there was no feeling in his body. The legs that moved woodenly didn't seem to be his.

Logan sprawled limp, the hand with the pocket pistol in it lying across his belly. Looking down at him, Brade asked, "Why?"

There was no answer. He knew there'd be none from Logan. Not ever again.

And suddenly, he knew that he had to get the hell away. He had to get himself out of here and hidden before the man at the door could discover him.

CHAPTER 14

As he turned, Brade felt pain. It started in his back, at the left shoulder blade. It grew, spreading until it filled his whole body. He stumbled toward the door and shoved it open.

He could hear sounds from the hallway below. Leaning against the wall, he wrapped his hand around the butt of the revolver that was still in his belt.

A small flame appeared at the foot of the stairs, giving shape to the hand that held the match. It rose toward a wall lamp, steadied, and caught.

He saw the man then. The lean, lanky man who'd gotten out of the carriage. Light washed the hawk face under the thatch of soot gray hair as the man turned to look up the staircase.

"Adam McCoy!" Brade's startled whisper was knife-sharp

in the stillness. His hand jerked the revolver, clearing his belt. He leveled it toward McCoy and called, "Don't move."

The man stood gazing up at him, obviously respecting the gun, but not looking afraid.

Cautiously, Brade took a step down the stairs. It felt like they swayed under him. He wanted to brace a hand against the wall, but his left arm was without feeling, as useless as if it were a log hung from his shoulder. He needed his right hand for the gun. Sinking his teeth into his lip, he fought pain with pain and tried for another step.

He'd gotten a little better than halfway down the staircase when the world rocked so suddenly that he had to lean against the banister to keep from falling. With stubborn determination, he kept the revolver leveled at McCoy.

"Who the devil are you? A robber?" McCoy asked him.

He almost grinned. If the damned ugly thought shaping itself in his mind was true, there was a cruel irony in that. He said, "This is *your* house?"

McCoy nodded.

"You are Bob Alan Logan's *friend* in St. Louis?"

Suspicion flashed in McCoy's face. He said nothing, but Brade felt certain of the answer.

"Adam McCoy, the fire-eating Reb-lyncher. *You're* the man we've been riding for—stealing and killing for!"

"You're one of Logan's bushwackers," McCoy said huskily. There was fear in his gaze now.

"Yeah. Lieutenant Caudell Prescott Bradenton, late of Todd's Irregulars," Brade told him in a voice colder than steel. There was strength in anger. It overrode the pain. "Caudell Prescott Bradenton, late of Bob Alan's Logan's damned double-crossed, misled fools."

"Look, Bradenton," McCoy gestured vaguely with one hand. His eyes held to the gun like a bird staring at a snake. "There's no need—you can—Logan's making good money for himself on this deal. You could, too. Riding for me, you can be a rich man."

"Riding to thieve from my own people? Riding to make them look like the kind of murderers you claim them to be?"

"The Confederacy is *dead!"* McCoy snapped. "The Rebs are traitors to the nation. They deserve punishment. Why shouldn't we make a profit on it? When I'm governor of Missouri, we'll pick their bones. Plenty in it for everyone. Don't be a fool, Bradenton. You can share in the profit."

"I'm a Reb. It's *my* bones you want to pick."

"No! Look, boy, you can forget that. Change—"

"Like a snake changes its skin?"

"What *do* you want?"

"I've made a bad mistake. I got to straighten it up as best I can," Brade said slowly. The stairs under him were swaying again. The gun was a heavy, trembling weight in his hand. As he gazed down the barrel, trying to steady it, McCoy's image blurred. Brade could still feel the anger, but the strength it had brought was flickering out. He tightened his finger on the trigger.

His hand wouldn't hold steady. The gun jerked as the scear released. And Adam McCoy threw himself down. Lead tore futilly into the wall as the jolt of the blast snatched the revolver out of Brade's hand.

The world pinwheeled, sliding from under him. His legs buckled, and he was falling. Cursing and tumbling, falling into eternity.

He fought desperately against the darkness that tried to wrap itself over him. With a terrible slowness, the spinning eased. The world righted itself.

He knew he was lying face down against soft carpeting. Squinting open his eyes, he saw lamplight through his lashes. The eternity of tumbling had only been a moment or so, he thought. But it had been time enough for Adam McCoy.

McCoy stood between him and the lamp, with the light falling across his shoulder, gleaming on the double-barreled hideout gun he held. Through slitted eyes, Brade could see the thumb tug back the hammer.

The door behind McCoy swung open with a sudden startling crash, slamming into the wall.

McCoy wheeled. His pistol leveled toward the man standing in the doorway.

Brade recognized Orin Coleman. Motionless, he stared at the man.

"You too!" McCoy grunted. He sounded as happy as a spider with a fresh-caught fly. "This *is* convenient."

Struggling for the strength, Brade snaked a hand toward the revolver he'd dropped. He saw Coleman blink, the pale eyes flicking toward him, then back to McCoy. Trying hard for blank innocence, Coleman said, "What's happening? I heard shots."

"You're going to hear more," McCoy smirked.

Brade's hand closed on the butt of the gun. Shifting slightly, he edged up the muzzle. He couldn't sight it, but he was too close to miss. *If* he could get the heavy hammer back.

His forefinger was tight on the trigger. His thumb hauled back against the hammer. His teeth dug into his lip, and the taste of blood filled his mouth.

The action yielded stiffly. The hammer moved. The ratchet

stuttered faintly as the cylinder turned, bringing a fresh cap and charge under the hammer.

Coleman was saying something, stalling and holding McCoy's attention. Brade didn't hear the words, but he was aware of the growing despair in Coleman's voice. He knew that in a moment, McCoy would fire. One barrel for Coleman, then the other for him.

He felt the hammer slipping under his thumb. It slid out of his grip. The gun bucked, spewing flame and smoke. The roar almost drowned McCoy's startled scream.

Through the haze, he saw McCoy half turn and hang poised at an impossibly awkward angle. The hawk face twisted, flesh drawing taut over sharp bone. The mouth gaped open. Blood spurted from it, a gush of thick dark blood that flooded down the chin. It spilled onto the white ruffles of McCoy's shirt and dribbled onto the floor.

McCoy leaned, seeming to look down. He toppled to lie with arms and legs askew. His back heaved, his whole body shuddered, and then he was still.

Coleman's face was pale as he knelt to touch the body. He spoke with hushed awe. "Dead."

For a moment, Brade let his head rest against his arm. But he knew he couldn't stay where he was. Drawing a deep breath, he looked at Coleman.

There were still loads in the revolver, and it was still in Brade's hand. Bracing himself, he managed to sit up. The pain flared fresh in his injured shoulder. Fighting to ignore it, he aimed the gun toward Coleman.

"What the hell are you doing here?"

"Heard shooting," Coleman muttered, watching him with strangely hooded eyes.

A sound from the back of the house cut raggedly across Brade's awareness. McCoy's manservant coming to investigate? He put his thumb to the gun hammer. With a jerk of his wrist, he used the weight of the gun against the spring. The hammer came back under his thumb, clicking loud as the scear caught. He said, "Got to get out of here. You've got to help me."

Coleman understood that click. Eyeing the cocked revolver, he got to his feet and held a hand toward Brade. There was no way to keep the gun pointed at him and accept his help, but Brade clung to it as he got his arm over Coleman's shoulder.

The noises from the back became more distinct. Hesitant footsteps. A voice called tentatively, "Mister McCoy?"

"Quick, dammit!" Brade whispered harshly.

Half dragging him, Coleman hurried for the door. Outside,

they ducked into the shadows of the hedge. Kneeling, hanging onto Coleman, Brade saw a man look furtively through the doorway, hesitate, then scurry down the stairs and across the yard to the next house. He hammered at the door.

It opened, and he disappeared inside. As soon as he was gone, Brade snapped to Coleman, "Got to get away from here."

Obediently, Coleman helped him to his feet again. They cut alongside McCoy's house and across backyards. The ground heaved under Brade's feet. He could feel the darkness closing in thickly around him. It tried to mire him. Step after step, staggering, he fought against it.

Suddenly, there was a thought clear in his mind. He stopped. Thin-voiced, he said, "Where you headed? Where you think you're taking me?"

"I know a surgeon not too far from here."

"Surgeon?" The last time a surgeon had laid hands on him, he'd been a prisoner and close to hanging. How close was he to it now? He mumbled, "No surgeon."

"You need one. You've been shot."

"I'll heal."

"I think you've still got the bullet in you. Maybe broken bone. Maybe pieces of cloth and trash in the wound. You ever heard of sepsis? Want gangrene?"

"Had gangrene. Don't like it. Don't like surgeons either." He grimaced, trying to force his thoughts into clear shape. "Who are you? A Pinkerton?"

"No, and I'm not the law either," Coleman answered. "This surgeon's a friend of mine. You can trust him. You've got my word on that."

"Can't trust *you.*"

"You've got to. Come on, you want to stand here and bleed to death?"

Brade sighed. He could feel the gun still in his hand, but it was damned small comfort. Hurt and halfway unconscious, he needed Coleman's help. He knew that much.

"I got your word? No law?" he mumbled.

"You've got my word," Coleman said. "No law. At least, not for now."

"All right." Brade's voice was barely a whisper. He felt the darkness closing in on him again. Coleman started to move. Hanging on, he staggered through black eternities.

Suddenly, he was awake. He was lying face down in the billowy softness of a feather bed. Motionless, he considered. It felt as if there were bandages wrapped around his chest and over his shoulder. The pain was still there, but faint now.

Opening his eyes slightly, he saw sunlight beaming through glass windows. It didn't seem to be a jail or a hospital, but a bedroom. Tilting his head, he spotted Coleman sprawled in an armchair near the foot of the bed. It looked like he was asleep. Brade's revolver lay in his lap, his fingers loose around the butt.

Cautiously, Brade shifted onto his side. His left arm was in a sling. He found he could move it, though it stirred fresh pain in his back. The bandages didn't hinder him much, and the pain wasn't intense enough to stop him. He sat up on the edge of the bed. For a moment, he was giddy, but it passed. He knew he had strength enough to move. To travel, if he had to. He glanced at Coleman, wondering.

Rising, he went silently to the window and looked out. He seemed to be on the second floor of a private house. Across the yard, he saw a stable.

"Thinking of leaving?"

He turned toward Coleman. The man's face was bland, softened by a light beard stubble. The pale eyes were red-rimmed and sleepy-looking, but they weren't blankly disinterested. Hot fires burned in them. The hand closed on the gun butt.

"Suppose you start by telling me abut this conspiracy of McCoy's with Logan and your bunch," he said.

Brade seated himself on the bed. "Suppose I don't?"

"Dammit, man, you know you're in trouble. I can help you. I can make it a lot easier for you if you'll talk."

Shrugging, Brade said innocently, "Me? In trouble?"

Coleman sighed. Watching from under half-closed lids, he muttered, "You're the one I can't make any sense of. I've got a clear picture of what McCoy and Logan were up to. But *you,* Bradenton—I talked to people in Lafayette County about you. For a bushwacker, you've got a good reputation. Even the charcoals around there give you grudging respect as an honest man. How the hell'd you come to turn coat and throw in with McCoy's conspiracy?"

"You got some kind of proof that I've been mixed up with McCoy?"

"I was following Logan's trail. I was able to see what he was doing." He spoke with a mock patience, spelling it all out. "He and a couple of others were traveling around together, contacting ex-bushwackers. I caught up with them at Lexington. I was following them when they burned your place. I lost Logan again, but—"

"When they *what!*"

"Burned your place," Coleman eyed him thoughtfully. "You didn't know about that?"

He shook his head. He'd never even thought of it. But now it made sense. Logan had done it to get him riled enough at the jayhawkers to be willing to ride and fight again. But what the devil was Coleman's part in all this?

He asked, "How come you to be trailing Logan?"

"You've heard of Judge Daniel Carlisle?"

That name had been in the newspapers a lot a while back. Judge Carlisle had been one of the reunionists who'd wanted to get the mess left by the war cleaned up and the ex-Rebs reenfranchised. He'd fought the charcoals at every turn. He'd been a man with influence, and the Rebs in Missouri had put a lot of hope in him.

"A good man," he muttered. "Only he died too soon."

"He was murdered," Coleman's voice was suddenly hard and harsh. "By Bob Alan Logan."

"Huh?"

"I worked for Judge Carlisle. Had read law under him. I was in the house when it happened—almost saw it—did see the man who did it. Bob Alan Logan."

"You were hunting him to kill him?" Brade asked, but he didn't think that was the reason. Coleman'd had his chances at Logan.

"No, I was following him to find out who paid him to murder the judge. It was planned to look like an interrupted burglary. That's the way it went on the records, but it was a political assassination. I was certain of that. I had to find out who was behind it. I wanted proof."

"McCoy was behind it?" Brade asked.

Coleman nodded.

"You got proof?"

"I have now. You and Logan led me to him. Now that he's dead, it'll be easier." Coleman paused. "Why'd he shoot you?"

"Wasn't McCoy. It was Logan. I guess he realized I'd find out about McCoy. He knew I'd figure out we'd been double-crossed."

"How's that?"

Hesitating, Brade considered. With what Coleman knew already, it wasn't going to do any good to deny the truth. He answered, "The way Logan laid it out for us, we thought we were helping the Reb cause. We thought we were fighting *against* McCoy."

"By robbing banks and raiding towns bushwacker style? That's pretty hard to swallow."

"Maybe some rats are too smart to take a poison bait, but

I reckon I ain't. You get hungry enough, though, you can swallow a damned lot of things."

"Hungry for what? Money?"

He shook his head. "Not money. Rights. You take away a man's lawful rights, tell him he can't vote or have a say in things, tell him he can't get caught carrying a gun even for hunting, and you start putting taxes to him and shoving him around like he wasn't a man at all but some kind of animal you held title to, he gets hungry to fight back. He gets a notion to do damned near anything that might make a change. If the only way of fighting he knows is with a gun, that's the way he'll do it. Logan knew that. He made us to think it'd work. He said he had a friend in St. Louis who had influence and could use the raiding and the money to twist up Jeff City and get us rid of the charcoals. I reckon we swallowed the bait whole."

"You didn't know his *friend* was Adam McCoy?"

"Hell no! You think if we'd had a notion of it, we wouldn't have sent him back Logan weighted with lead?"

For a long moment, Coleman studied him through half-closed eyes. Slowly, with conviction, he said, "You're telling me the truth."

Brade nodded.

"Well, Logan is dead, and McCoy is dead," Coleman muttered, starting to his feet. "And I've got enough now to have an official investigation started. We'll destroy what's left of McCoy's organization within the government. Once you've testified—"

"Hold on!" Brade snapped, rising to face him. "You ain't getting *me* to testify to anything."

"There'll be an inquest about McCoy's death. You'll have to appear."

"No sir! Not and get hauled into court for the killing. You know damned well that under charcoal law, there can't anybody set a jury here now except Yankee sympathizers. I'm a *bushwacker*. I been lieutenant to George Todd. You haul *me* up in front of a jury like that, they'll hang me first and try me afterward."

Coleman looked uncertain. He began, "You've broken the law. You've been robbing banks—"

"You sure of that?" Brade said slowly. He was almost grinning at the thought that had taken shape for him. "You say you've read law. Can you swear. . . ?" He paused, hunting the phrase he wanted. "Can you swear of your own knowledge that I done anything except break parole to carry a gun and shoot McCoy to save *your* life? You got any *proof* I ever robbed a bank?"

"Huh?" Coleman flinched as if he'd been slapped in the face. Finally, he gave a very slow shake of his head. "No, not of my own knowledge. Not *proof*."

"You know of anybody who can swear to it?"

"No."

"Can you say I didn't have cause to shoot McCoy? You figure I done wrong killing him to stop him of killing you?"

"No," Coleman owned reluctantly.

"Then if the law hanged me, it wouldn't be for a murder or a bank robbery. It'd be because I'd fought under George Todd. They *told* me we'd got amnesty for that."

Turning away from him, Coleman walked to the window and looked out. Brade eyed the revolver still in his hand, thinking he could move behind Coleman's back and take it away. But he had a feeling he didn't need to. He waited.

Softly, Coleman said, "You may be right about that Yankee jury."

"You know damn well I'm right."

Coleman wheeled. He flung the gun down on the bed. "I guess I can get the investigation rolling without your testimony. A lawyer has an obligation to protect a client."

Scooping up the gun, Brade shoved it into his belt.

"War's sure made a mess of things," Coleman mumbled to himself. He looked at Brade again. "As your lawyer, I'd recommend you get the hell out of Missouri—and stay out."

"I've heard there's a lot of good farmland west of Missouri," Brade answered, grinning. He thought of the stop-off he'd have to make on his way west. Amy'd be waiting for him. He was certain of it. She'd laugh and tease and give him hell for getting a bullet hole in his coat. But when she did, he'd promise never to let it happen again.